"I KEPT TRYING TO BREAK IT OFF," she said. "Friday night—the night he was killed—I was with him, and I told him I wanted to end it. But he kept . . . pushing. That was the last time I saw him. You see, it was just because I was so lonely. It was stupid of me, I know. You have to believe me."

She turned back to Sam, and he saw that she was in pain.

"I never, never loved him," she added.

Sam felt a great sense of relief. "All right," he said, trying to comfort Brooke. "Then what are you so frightened of?"

Brooke gestured helplessly, as if she wanted to tell him but could not. She asked, "You don't think I did it—killed him—do you?"

ROY SCHEIDER   MERYL STREEP

"STILL OF THE NIGHT"

JESSICA TANDY

Director of Photography
NESTOR ALMENDROS, A.S.C.

Screenplay by
ROBERT BENTON

Story by
DAVID NEWMAN and ROBERT BENTON

Produced by
ARLENE DONOVAN

Directed by
ROBERT BENTON

TECHNICOLOR®

PANAVISION®

Rated PG

Distributed by
MGM/UA
Entertainment Co.

STILL OF
THE NIGHT

A novel by Robert Alley

From the screenplay
by Robert Benton

Story by David Newman and Robert Benton

BALLANTINE BOOKS • NEW YORK

Library of Congress Catalog Card Number: 82-90869

ISBN 0-345-30689-9

Manufactured in the United States of America

First Edition: December 1982

Cover photograph by Henry Wolf.

1

The full moon touched the rooftops of upper Manhattan with a cold, clear light.

Corridors of elegant brownstones running east from Fifth Avenue, away from the park and the Metropolitan Museum of Art, produced their own brilliance, as street lamps and bright windows resisted the darkness. The neighborhood seemed free of any threat, a refuge where wealth was reflected not just in the size and beauty of the houses, the well-tended trees, and wrought-iron railings, but also in the gleaming hoods of cars parked tightly to each curb. They were foreign and domestic, triumphs of design, ready to whisk their owners to any part of the vast city, and each of them was worth a small fortune.

A lone figure strolled into the glare of an antique shop, then paused to light a cigarette. The flame of the gold Ronson revealed a full, dark mustache and a youthful, handsome face. The man wore a tailored leather jacket and Gucci shoes, so that a casual passerby might have mistaken him for a resident of one of the townhouses. Instead, he was a thief—an accomplished one. He was not interested in the matching Ming vases or the Chip-

1

pendale chairs on the other side of the plate glass, but in the Mercedes, the BMW, and the Cadillac, all within easy reach. If just one of them was unlocked, within an hour he would deliver it to a garage in Queens, where the serial number would be ground away and the license plates and the color changed.

He stepped into the street. Drawing casually on his cigarette, he backed up against the Seville and tried the door. It was locked. He moved on to the Porsche, whose loving owner had placed a decal on the window advising that the car was equipped with an alarm. The thief tried the Mercedes 190SL instead, but it too resisted him. He quickly crossed the street, walking between a Lincoln and an aging Jaguar, jerking hard on the handle of the first car. It was as tight as a bank vault.

He cursed softly to himself. What had seemed promising territory when he first started down the street had produced nothing. There was a chance that he had already been seen, that an emergency call had gone out. A police cruiser could be speeding up Madison Avenue at that moment; it was dangerous to try more than a few cars on any street.

He turned to the Jaguar. It was painted black and in need of a wash job; something about the car bothered him, but he did not have time to figure out what. He sidled up to the driver's door, pulled the handle, and this time felt the satisfying release of the latch. He opened the door, and a man fell backward into the street. The thief looked down at the contorted face and bulging eyes of what he thought was a drunk. Then he saw that the man's

2

throat had been hideously slashed and was smeared with blood.

A hand, stiff with rigor mortis, brushed against the thief's new trousers. The gaping mouth of the dead man seemed about to speak to him. Terrified, he clung to the car door, trying to force it closed again, gasping for breath.

He ran blindly toward the park.

Detective First Class Joseph Vitucci had been trained to deal with murder. He had seen people killed with guns, lengths of pipe, knotted rope, and even strychnine, but it was the knives that bothered him the most. They produced a sense of horror in the victims that remained mirrored in their faces long after death. Looking down at the corpse sprawled on the pavement, Vitucci wondered at the cruelty required to inflict such wounds.

He stepped aside to let the technicians from Forensic into the victim's car. It was a beautiful October morning, too early for traffic, yet already warmed by the sun. Police cars blocked both ends of the street, and two vans belonging to local television stations—Channel Five and Channel Nine— were parked side by side, the competing cameramen shouldering their equipment for long shots of the murder scene. Two uniformed policemen stood in the door of the brownstone behind Vitucci, taking a statement from the woman who had discovered the body, a middle-aged executive, who had come out at dawn to walk her yellow Labrador; it would be a long time before she slept soundly again.

A group of residents stood across the street, silently watching the investigators. They all looked well-heeled to Vitucci, and fearful; Vitucci couldn't blame them. He had grown up in Washington Heights, where crime was common, and had put himself through college in one long, hungry struggle; but that didn't mean he couldn't sympathize with rich people who woke up to find a corpse on their sidewalk. Murder was an outrage to society in general. That was one of the first thing he had learned at the Police Academy.

One technician went over the front seat of the Jaguar with a hand-held vacuum cleaner, ignoring the body, searching for scraps of evidence. A team at Forensic would pass the contents of the bag beneath a microscope later in the day. While he worked, the van from the morgue backed up over the curb and two men came toward Vitucci, one of them carrying a body bag. Chalk lines had already been drawn on the pavement, and photographs taken. The men spread the bag and casually lifted the body onto it; Vitucci took a final look before they zipped him up. The victim was a good-looking middle-aged guy with salt-and-pepper hair and natty clothes. He had not been robbed, which made the case more interesting. The murderer had been able to get quite close to the victim and to strike at will. Judging from the savagery and the number of the wounds, the murderer had been either extremely angry or extremely frightened.

The other technician from Forensic sprayed the inside of the car—steering wheel, dashboard, door panels, and windows—with a new chemical used to lift fingerprints. Vitucci was about to tell him to spray the back seat, too, when he was distracted by the sound of a siren. The small crowd at the end of the block made way for another squad car, assuming it contained someone important. Vitucci knew the squad car contained his breakfast.

The men from the morgue lifted the body into the van, and Murray, the coroner's assistant, ambled up to the detective. His badge was pinned high on his lab technician's coat, proving that he represented the Chief Medical Officer. Murray wore thick glasses with heavy black rims, and his smile contained too many teeth. He was always challenging Vitucci's findings in murder cases, and suggesting different conclusions. The trouble was Murray was sometimes right, and Vitucci wrong.

"Okay," Murray said, taking out his pad. "What's the victim's name?"

"Bynum," Vitucci told him. "George Bynum."

The squad car had reached the murder scene; the siren and the revolving red light died together. The young cop climbed out of the driver's seat with a gray metal box that usually contained the evidence and hurried toward Detective First Class Vitucci.

"Sir . . ." he began.

But Vitucci had to spell out Bynum's name for Murray, who was more adept at evaluating evidence than at distinguishing among vowels and consonants. One thing Vitucci had learned at City University was how to spell.

"B-y-n-u-m."

"Sir . . ."

"Just a second," Vitucci told Murray. He had hoped the cop would wait until Murray was gone. "What is it, officer?"

5

"They didn't have the jelly donuts, so I got you a French cruller. Is that all right?"

Murray snorted in amusement as the cop opened the gray box and revealed an assortment of Styrofoam coffee cups and glazed pastries.

"Okay," Vitucci said, "which is the light with extra sugar?"

The patrolman handed him the appropriate container and a pastry wrapped in wax paper.

"Gimme a regular," said Murray, getting in on the act. He took his coffee as if it was his due and leaned against the fender of the dead man's car. He set the cup on the hood and took a plastic bag from the pocket of his coat. Inside the bag was a wad of money.

"He had two hundred and twenty-seven dollars and change on him." Murray thrust the bag toward Vitucci, who was savoring the sticky sweetness of his warm cruller. "Count it."

"Now, Murray, I trust you."

Murray shrugged. He placed the money on the hood, next to his coffee. He offered Vitucci his pad and the list of the victim's possessions to read. He did, swallowing most of the cruller, and then signed the list.

"You shouldn't eat that stuff," Murray said. "It's poison."

Nice thought, Vitucci said to himself. Very tasteful. He shoved the rest of the cruller into his mouth as Murray tore off a copy of the list and handed it across, along with the plastic bag. He started to leave, then turned back toward Vitucci.

"Five bucks says this guy's a repeater."

Vitucci's mouth was full. "C'mon, Murray, how

6

can you say that?" Murray's snap judgments annoyed him. "You can't say that."

Murray was only too happy to prove that he could say it.

"What does it take to kill a guy?" he asked. "Three stab wounds? Maybe four, tops. Right?"

Vitucci wouldn't give him the satisfaction of answering.

"Am I right?"

"You're right, Murray."

"All right, now. Just from what I saw here, I count nine, ten wounds minimum." Murray assumed a studious expression that by now was familiar to Vitucci: it was Murray's armchair-psychiatrist look. "That's a lot of anger," he went on. "That's a lot of rage that's been held in check for a long time. I'll tell you one thing, now it's out in the open, it's not gonna be so easy for this guy to stop."

"Yeah?" In spite of himself, Vitucci felt a chill. One murder like this was too much.

"I'm telling you," said Murray, as cheerful as ever. "You got a repeater, pal."

Vitucci took the bet.

2

The predictable, ordered life of Dr. Samuel Rice was reflected in his office. A large, pleasant room with a distant view of the Fifty-ninth Street Bridge, it contained Danish modern furniture—all blond wood and muted colors—and a meticulously selected library of books dealing with psychiatry. On the wall hung a watercolor landscape and several diplomas. Patients' files were neatly arranged on the bottom shelf of the bookcase. His pencils, freshly sharpened after each appointment, lay side by side on his desk. Also on the desk stood a telephone, a ceramic statue of a Greek goddess, and an empty ashtray.

He sat behind the desk in his professional pose, elbows on the armrests of his swivel chair, fingertips pressed together. Although in his mid-forties, Sam had a lean athlete's body and greying hair. Glasses with clear plastic rims offset the boyishness of a frank, open face, one that naturally inspired people to confide in him.

Sam listened attentively to his patient, a paunchy senior executive in a large advertising firm who was stretched out on the couch. The man's tie was undone, and he stared at the ceiling with wide, desperate eyes. "I don't understand what happened,"

9

the patient was saying. "I mean it, that account was practically mine. Then that son of a bitch comes in and stabs"—the man's hand shot forward, as if it contained a knife; Sam winced—"and stabs me in the back."

Sam experienced a rush of sorrow and disgust. He wrote the word *Hostility* on his stenographer's pad. Everything his patients said was tape-recorded in the office, so Sam could go over the words at his leisure and strengthen his analyses. He jotted notes to himself, reminders of a patient's attitude and behavior. Sam was having difficulty concentrating.

"And do you want to know what the reason is?" the executive asked. Sam did not want to know; he wanted to know what the executive *thought* the reason was. "I'll tell you what the reason is. It's because he plays the company game; that's what the reason is."

Suddenly the man began to cry. He plucked a Kleenex from the box that Sam had placed beside him on the floor and dabbed at his eyes.

"I'm not kidding," he went on. "I think I honestly deserved to be president."

He obviously wanted Sam to agree, but he remained silent. It had taken Sam years to develop his professional detachment.

"Don't you think I *deserved* to be president?"

"Would it make you feel any better," Sam asked, "if I told you that you did?"

"Yeah, sure." He turned his head and grinned at Sam. "You bet!"

Sam could have obliged, but that would not help the patient. Eventually the man would have to realize that he invited others to take advantage of him, that he actually expected to fail.

"I'm sorry this happened to you," Sam told him. "But have you thought about why this sort of thing keeps happening to you?" The time was up. "I think this is something we should get into next week."

The man lay there for a moment longer, collecting himself. Then he sat up, took a deep breath, and swung his feet to the floor. Obviously exhausted, he stood and walked out into the waiting room, leaving the door ajar.

Sam switched off the tape recorder. His thoughts were with another patient, George Bynum, whose picture had been plastered across the front page of the *Daily News*. His murder had shocked Sam, and he felt partly responsible, as any good psychiatrist would. Obviously there were important aspects of Bynum's life that Sam had been unable to bring to the surface. Bynum was the first patient of Sam's to meet a violent death, reminding Sam that beyond the door of his well-ordered office lay an unpredictable and sometimes dangerous world.

He punched the button on his answering machine. Another patient had called to request an appointment. Then Sam heard the voice of his wife, Sarah, say, "Hello, dear. I'm just calling to tell you that the divorce is final. The lawyer and I—"

Sam jabbed the button, cutting her off in midsentence. He didn't want to hear the details. He had not wanted a divorce in the first place and had been shocked when Sarah brought it up. For all his intuitive ability and his scholarship, Sam had been unable to foresee the deterioration of his own marriage and Sarah's discontent. He had always been careful not to bore her with the problems of his patients, but she considered that secretive. It was life itself that bored her, a doctor's life, with its rigorous scheduling, the long hours spent over the desk at home, the distraction of patients calling with their own problems, the constant analysis. Every time they disagreed, whether on the subject of a weekend retreat or which play to see, Sarah would end up saying, "Stop analyzing me, for Christ's sake!" He had never really analyzed her, though someone should. Sam wondered how he would appear in Sarah's confessions to another psychiatrist. "You're nice looking, and you're good in bed," she had told him. "But you've never taken a chance in your life. Everything you do and think is so perfectly *safe*, Sam."

His gaze wandered to the bookshelf. There among the works of Freud and Jung were half a dozen books on baseball. An old New York Yankees cap and two autographed baseballs sat on the shelf below. Baseball had been a passion with him. He had once wanted to play professionally instead of studying psychology, but reason had prevailed. Now Sam wondered why he kept that junk around his office.

He went over and picked up the soggy Kleenex left by the patient on the couch. He carried it and the ashtray full of cigarette butts into the adjoining bathroom and dropped them into the toilet. He flushed it. The sound of running water drowned out a woman's voice. Someone had entered his office and spoken his name, and Sam turned to see a beautiful blonde standing in the middle of his beige carpet, watching him. Her hair, parted in the middle, fell smoothly to her shoulders, framing a face with high cheekbones and a lovely, aquiline nose. Her lips, parted in an uncertain smile, were a deep red; her blue eyes had a depthless, haunted quality. Sam found himself oddly speechless.

"Doctor Rice?" she repeated.

He nodded, going out to her. The tailored black coat lent her an air of austerity; he detected the barest trace of expensive perfume.

"Your door was open, so I . . ." She faltered, and Sam recognized a familiar sign of stress. She seemed to gather her courage, and said, "My name is Brooke Reynolds."

He tried to conceal his surprise. The name was also familiar to him, so familiar that Sam had invented a person to go with it, one that bore little resemblance to the real thing. Brooke Reynolds had played a significant role in the analysis of George Bynum, the murder victim. Bynum had had an affair with her, and had told his psychiatrist all about it, occasionally taunting Sam with the suggestion that the young woman would also find him attractive. Sam had pictured someone with a brassy sexiness and less intelligence and style. Looking at the real Brooke Reynolds, Sam's opinion of the dead man went up several notches.

"Ah . . ." He didn't know exactly how to begin.

"I was a friend of George Bynum," she said, as if to get that on the record. "I was wondering if I could talk to you for a moment." Her cheeks were deeply flushed. "I promise I won't take long."

"Certainly."

13

Sam motioned her toward a chair and took his seat behind the desk. He felt more comfortable in a professional pose. Brooke sat down and immediately began to rummage through her pocketbook. The death of Bynum had obviously left her distraught, and Sam had to be careful how he dealt with her. Brooke Reynolds was not his patient; he knew nothing about her, other than what Bynum had told him, and that may or may not have been the truth. She was, Sam realized, a possible suspect in an investigation that had already found its way to Sam's office.

"I need you to help me," said Brooke. "The last time I saw George, he left this in my apartment."

She took a watch from her handbag and placed it on the desk. She gently shoved it across toward Sam, who made no move to take it.

"Before I had a chance to return it, I heard that he had been . . ." She faltered again, embarrassed by her own nervousness. ". . . that he was dead."

She pushed the watch closer to Sam.

"I thought his wife would want it."

He picked up the watch. It was a classic Cartier, with a dark lizard-skin band. On the back were inscribed the words: TO GEORGE, FROM HIS LOVING WIFE. Sam wondered if Bynum's loving wife knew about all his philandering.

Brooke took a crumpled pack of Gauloise cigarettes from her purse. "Do you mind if I smoke?"

"No, not at all."

She inserted a cigarette between her lips, avoiding looking into Sam's eyes. It took three matches to get the cigarette lit. Her pale, slender hands shook.

"I don't know her," Brooke said of Bynum's wife, then contradicted herself. "Well, we've met once or twice. . . . What I'm trying to say is that I don't think she knows anything about George and me. And there's no reason why she should be hurt by this, now."

Sam said nothing. He knew the professional value of silence in drawing out a patient's thoughts, and he was unsure of his own response. This young woman seemed sincere and was undeniably attractive, but her behavior was suspicious, to say the least. She was correct in wanting to protect the dead man's wife from added grief, but what were Brooke Reynolds's motives?

"If you could return the watch to her," Brooke said, "and not say anything about me . . ." Sam's reticence added to her nervousness. "I thought you could say that he left it here the last time he came for a session . . . or something."

"I was sorry to hear about George," said Sam, relenting. "When this sort of thing happens, I know . . ."

But she wasn't interested in his professional opinion. Interrupting him, she demanded, "Doctor Rice, what did he tell you about me?"

So that was it. She wanted to know what her dead lover thought of her.

"What makes you think he told me anything about you?"

"When I told you my name," she said, "it was obvious you knew who I was." So much for Sam's professionalism; he couldn't even hide his emotions from a stranger. "George and I had an affair. He

15

must have told you something about me. I think I have a right to know what it was."

"Miss Reynolds, anything that is said between a doctor and his patient is privileged."

She shook her head vehemently. "You don't understand. I don't care about George"—the unexpected confession surprised him; he also felt an unexpected sense of relief—"the details of his analysis, I mean. All I care about are the things he said about me, personal things that belong to me."

Why did she want to know what Bynum had said about her if she didn't really care for him?

"I can't," he said simply.

"But that's not fair!" She seemed more hurt than angry, grinding out her cigarette in the heavy onyx ashtray. "Why?"

"It may not be fair, but I really can't help you."

She leaned across his desk and said pleadingly, in a girl's voice, "Please."

Sam would never make an exception to professional ethics. But he felt a strong, admittedly irrational urge to help this beautiful young woman.

Before he could respond, the intercom on the wall buzzed. Grateful for this interruption, he said "Excuse me" and pushed the button beneath the speaker. "Yes?"

"Doctor Rice?" It was the policeman who had telephoned earlier. "This is Detective Joseph Vitucci, from Homicide. I called you about an appointment."

Brooke leapt up from the chair and, before Sam could answer the detective, lunged for the watch on his desk. Her hand accidentally struck the

16

statuette, and it fell against the ashtray, breaking. The tiny ceramic arm lay severed.

"Oh," she said, genuinely distressed. "I'm sorry."

Her agitation had also brought Sam to his feet. They had both forgotten the watch. "Don't worry about it."

"Can I pay you?"

"It's not important." He smiled, trying to calm her. "It gets broken once a month."

Brooke turned quickly away. She was concerned about more than the statuette. "This was stupid," she murmured. "Very stupid."

Sam carefully pushed the button on the intercom. "Could you step into the waiting room, please?" he asked the detective. "I'll be with you in a minute."

"I have to go," she said, desperate. She started to open the door, then stopped, realizing that the detective waited on the other side.

Sam stepped around the desk. He picked up the umbrella she had left next to her chair and handed it to her. "Here. You can use this door," he added, indicating the one that led directly to the hall.

She looked gratefully up at him. He opened the door, and she walked out quickly into the corridor. Sam wanted to say something reassuring.

"Miss Reynolds . . ."

She turned, but he couldn't think of anything. He was reluctant to see her go.

It was Brooke's turn to smile. "Thank you," she whispered, and then she was gone.

Sam returned to his desk, confused and somewhat elated. Both sensations were new to him. He realized that it had been months since he had responded so strongly to a woman. The smell of

17

Brooke's perfume lingered in the air like an admonition. He wondered if he should tell the detective about her visit and why he felt like protecting her.

He pushed the button on the intercom, and said, "Okay."

The detective entered with a note pad in hand. He wore a drab green suit and a tie with whales on it, but the NYPD-issue down vest that he wore underneath the jacket gave him an institutional look. He appeared younger than Sam, and eager. The psychiatrist could tell from the straight set of the detective's brows and narrow, canny eyes that he was tenacious, but not brilliant. Once Vitucci sunk his teeth in a case, however, he would not let go.

"Doctor Rice," he said, extending his hand, "I'm Joseph Vitucci, detective first class, Homicide Central. I appreciate your taking the time."

"Sure. Would you like to sit down?"

Vitucci pulled up the chair that Brooke had just vacated. Her cigarette smoldered in the ashtray. Vitucci put his note pad on the desk, inches from George Bynum's watch.

"You're a psychologist?" he asked.

"Psychiatrist."

Sam saw that the watch was turned face down. All the detective had to do was read the inscription.

"Oh, right," said Vitucci. He began to spell out the word *psychiatrist*, moving his lips as he wrote— "p-s-y-c-h-i-a . . ."

"That's right." Sam moved his hand toward the watch, but Vitucci looked up.

"And George Bynum was a patient of yours?"

"Yes."

"How long had you been treating him?"

"Twice a week for almost two years."

Vitucci returned to his note pad. Sam wanted to snatch the watch out of his line of vision, but that would be too obvious. He was sure Vitucci would notice the inscription and demand to know who had left the Gauloise in the ashtray before slipping out the back way. Sam wondered if he would tell him.

Vitucci asked, "And the last time you saw him?"

Sam took his appointment book from a drawer. It was real, lustrous leather—a gift from Sarah—and he opened it slowly and set it down on top of Bynum's Cartier.

"Thursday, October 22," he said, "at five-thirty in the afternoon."

"May I?"

Before Sam could protest, Vitucci had taken the book and turned it around so he could read the entry.

"The day before he died, right?"

"Yes," said Sam. The detective seemed to find that significant.

Vitucci closed the appointment book, revealing the watch.

"Now," he began, glancing at the watch without seeing the inscription. "Had anything unusual happened—threats, attempts on his life, etcetera? Anything like that that he might have mentioned to you?"

Sam shook his head.

"Anybody he was having trouble with?"

"Nothing," said Sam. With one easy motion he

19

reached across, palmed the watch, and dropped it into the open drawer. He smiled at the detective.

"What exactly were you treating the deceased for?" Vitucci asked.

Sam had been expecting the question. It was a natural one for a policeman to ask under the circumstances. Sam wanted to help in the investigation as much as he could, but there were limits to the usefulness of Bynum's psychiatric analysis. Sam felt no need to reveal information about the dead man that might cause added grief to his family and friends.

"You must understand," Sam said. "That's confidential information."

Vitucci seemed to accept that. There was an agreeableness about him unsuited to a pursuer of murderers. It occurred to Sam that Vitucci might be putting on a nice-guy act while keeping his real opinions and methods to himself.

"Listen," Vitucci said, "I don't know how it works exactly, the role of the psychiatrist, and the confidentiality issue, okay?" He shrugged, willing to be instructed. "What I mean is, I don't know if it's like a priest, or what."

While Vitucci had been speaking, Sam had noticed that the door behind him moved. Sam had not closed it securely after Brooke left. Now someone stood on the other side listening, unless the door had been moved by a current of air, which was unlikely. Sam sat and stared at it, deeply disturbed. If he stood up and flung the door open, he might find Brooke standing there.

Sam said amiably, "More or less." He didn't like to think of himself as a priest.

After a pause, Vitucci said, "Okay." He was giving up for the moment. He took out his wallet, extracted a card, and presented it to Sam. "If you can think of anything that's not confidential, and you feel you can tell me, I'd appreciate it if you'd give me a call. Okay?"

"Sure."

Sam stood up, glancing at the door. It had not moved again.

"Listen," said Vitucci, taking his time stuffing his wallet and note pad in his jacket pockets and rising with an effort. He would have been astounded if Sam had told him that his time was worth seventy-five dollars an hour. "If I were you, I'd be careful for the next couple of days. What I mean is, if *I* thought you might know something about George Bynum's death, then the guy who killed him might get the same idea."

"I will," Sam promised, but he was not really listening. He passed behind Vitucci's chair and casually opened the door.

The corridor was empty.

3

The clear, crisp autumn weather had not lasted. A steady rain was falling by the time Sam's last patient was done. Before leaving the office, Sam put George Bynum's folder and the tape recordings of his analytical sessions into his briefcase and rode down alone in the elevator. He caught a cab across town, part of the creeping, honking grid-lock caused by rain at rush hour; Sam paid little attention to the world beyond the car's flooded windows, or to the cabbie's monologue. He was thinking about the dead man. Somewhere among his recorded confessions, or among Sam's notes, might lie a clue to the identity of his killer. Sam could not release the information to the police, but he could assist by reviewing that information himself. Psychiatrists were investigators, after all. Maybe he could help Vitucci in his own way and satisfy his own sense of responsibility.

The cab labored up Broadway—past neighborhood liquor stores, cleaners, record shops, and storefronts covered with iron grates. He and Sarah had moved into an apartment on the upper West Side before Sam had begun to enjoy the affluence of an established psychiatrist, and they had stayed there even though they could have afforded living on the other side of Central Park. Moving was too distracting, Sam thought. He needed comfortable, familiar surroundings in which to live and work, although his wife took this as further evidence of his obsession with security. Maybe she was right.

He took the elevator to the sixth floor. Outside his apartment, Sam steeled himself against entering the empty rooms. He could not get used to the silences, after eight years of marriage. They had no children—it was Sarah's decision more than his own—but their life together had been rich and meaningful, or at least he thought so. He missed the companionship more than the sex.

Sam let himself in. The apartment was bright and airy, and as orderly as Sam's office. A Klee print greeted him in the hall, but the framed Ansel Adams photograph was gone, leaving a faded rectangle in its place. The living-room was lined with books, but there were large gaps on the shelves where Sarah had taken what she considered hers. For the same reason, the apartment was tastefully but only partially furnished: one wing chair instead of two, and only one reading lamp. The coffee table was gone. In the dining room, the exquisite early American sideboard gleamed in the light, but the refinished harvest table and the oak chairs had followed Sarah. Sam now had to get by with a card table and folding chairs.

Sam had been a contempoary anomaly—a happily married man. He and Sarah had a civilized marriage and, naturally, a civilized divorce. Standing there alone in the partially gutted apartment, he wished that he had raised more objections to splitting up, that he had done something uncivilized, like breaking a lamp or shouting at Sarah. Maybe that was what she really wanted, but it wasn't in Sam's nature to provide it. He had yet to face up to that failure.

He opened the briefcase and took out George Bynum's folder. He dropped it on the card table and went to pour himself some Tab. The freezer was stuffed with Stouffers dinners, but Sam was too preoccupied for a full meal. He quickly made a tunafish sandwich and carried it to the table.

Sam had many patients, being a popular psychiatrist; he could not always remember exactly what he had written about them. Sometimes he was surprised and delighted by his own insights, in light of what later analysis revealed. At other times his findings seemed uninspired, even petty. He was anxious to see what his initial impressions had been of Bynum, the well-dressed cataloguer of art and rare antiquities at Crispin's, the auction house.

Bynum had been referred by another patient of Sam's. Under the entry of January 4, Sam had written: "First session with George Bynum. Forty-seven, good health, works at Crispin's. He said the pre-Columbian statue on my desk was a cheap copy. Told me I watered my plants too much. Said he didn't really need to see me but was only doing it to please his wife. Finally admitted he was having trouble sleeping."

Sam remembered him as self-assured, irreverent, sometimes overbearing. He was compensating for some deficiency, but Sam had never discovered what that deficiency was. He apparently had no problems with women, favoring those with taste and sensibility. Like Brooke Reynolds.

Sam skipped a few pages. "It turns out," he had written a few weeks later, "that Bynum had been having an affair with one of the women at Crispin's. I gather these affairs happen with some frequency. This time his wife found out and threatened to go to his boss. The only way to pacify her was for Bynum to agree to see an analyst. It's not what you would call a promising start . . ."

The shriek of the doorbell interrupted him. Sam had always hated the sound of the thing and had planned to replace the device himself, but he had never gotten around to doing the job. Now it left him ill at ease. He was not expecting a visitor.

Slowly he walked to the door. He was probably one of the few people in Manhattan who did not have a peephole. He hesitated, then opened the door. In the dimly lighted corridor stood the familiar figure of his mother, her gray hair freshly and expertly set, her smile warm and expectant.

"I'm sorry I'm late," she said, brushing past him into the apartment. "I got a call from a patient, and . . ."

"Oh, my God," said Sam. They were both expected for dinner at Sam's uncle's house.

"You're not dressed!"

"Mother, I'm sorry. I just forgot."

She stared at him. They were both psychiatrists, and Sam's admission was full of hidden meaning. Freud said there is no such thing as a mistake. Particularly when you're dealing with your mother, Sam thought. She was an extremely successful analyst who was probably smarter than Sam, and certainly wiser. Sam could accept that with equanimity, but not for her efforts to analyze him.

The ash on her cigarette threatened to topple. She was as compulsively sloppy as Sam was neat, and harbored no guilt because of it. She walked into the living room, looking for an ashtray, which Sarah had no doubt taken with her, since Sam didn't smoke. His mother finally dumped her cigarette and ash into a potted jade tree and turned to face him.

She said simply, "Mmmmm."

"What's that supposed to mean?" Her name was Grace, but he never called her anything but Mother.

"It's supposed to mean *Mmmmm,* that's all."

She studied him, her chin in her hand, a characteristic pose. In spite of her age, Grace Rice was still an attractive woman, enhanced by her material success and the recognition given her by other professionals in the field. She had been a liberated woman long before the idea became politically fashionable. She wore designer clothes and moved with absolute assurance through any social scene; but she was also sentimental and ultimately indifferent to her appearance and surroundings. Her fashionable coat, for example, carried a smudge of cigarette ash on the lapel. But her intense, bright green eyes were the focus.

"It's not like you," she said, weighing the symptoms, "to forget Uncle Charlie's birthday. You're his favorite."

Sam was not really Uncle Charlie's favorite. It was amazing how family clichés endured over the years. Uncle Charlie thought psychiatrists were all quacks, Sam included.

"I had a lot of work to do," Sam said, hoping she would accept the excuse but knowing she would not. He had never been good at hiding things from her.

"Sam, is something wrong?"

"No," he insisted, "I'm fine."

She strolled around the room, looking at the places where furniture should have been. "Have you heard from Sarah lately?" she asked breezily.

"Yeah." Sam couldn't keep a trace of bitterness out of his voice. "She called to say the divorce is final."

"Mmmmm."

"Now do me a favor, don't start in on all that *Mmmmm* stuff."

It had irritated him for as long as he could remember. Grace had always switched effortlessly between the maternal and the professional; Sam was never sure which mode she was in. Trying to figure that out had exhausted him as a younger man and probably had a lot to do with his own decision to become a psychiatrist. That, and Grace's constant encouragement and love.

"Look," he added apologetically, "just tell Uncle Charlie I'm sorry that I couldn't come."

"Oh, come on. Uncle Charlie's not so bad." She smiled up at him, a little too insistent, while fishing another cigarette from her purse. "You never can tell who you'll meet."

So that was it! Sam's irritation returned; this time his mother had gone too far.

"All right," he demanded, "who is she?"

"Who is *who*?" Her feigned innocence was so transparent that Sam wanted to laugh. It was amazing how the best-trained psychiatrist could use the most childish evasions when avoiding the truth.

"Who's the woman at Uncle Charlie's?" Sam asked. "The one you're trying to fix me up with."

Grace lit her cigarette and nervously dropped the match on the rug. "I don't know what you're talking about."

"Let's see," he began speculatively, as if he were solving some problem of great neurological significance. "She's about thirty-five years old, widowed or divorced, with a couple of kids and a terrific sense of humor." He had been through it all before.

Grace stopped the pretense. "I don't see what harm there is in your meeting someone. How long has it been since you've gone out and seen people?"

"Mother," he said, trying to be reasonable, "I appreciate what you're trying to do, but I don't need a social director."

"All right, Sam." Suddenly she was all business. "What's wrong?"

"I lost a patient," he admitted.

"What happened?"

"A man named George Bynum. It was all over the *Daily News*."

Grace nodded, recognizing the name.

"He was stabbed to death," Sam said.

"That's awful." Her concern for Bynum quickly passed. "How are *you* taking it?"

"A lot better than he is."

"Sam, you mustn't blame yourself. You know as well as I do, no doctor is omniscient."

Grace tended to get involved in the lives and problems of her patients, while Sam avoided involvement. He favored the scholarly approach, which he thought was more beneficial to the patient in the end. Grace floundered in the emotions, yet was capable of absolute detachment when it was necessary.

"Forget omniscience," he said. "I'd settle for a batting average of two twenty-five." That also applied to his personal life unfortunately. "I never helped Bynum. To tell you the truth, I think he would have been a hell of a lot better off going to a priest or a rabbi . . ."

"Sam," Grace said gently. That admission was blasphemy, coming from a psychiatrist.

"I mean it. He should have, instead of paying seventy-five dollars an hour to some doctor who can't even keep his own marriage together."

That was too much for her. "Now you listen to me. I'm not talking mother to son; I'm talking shrink to shrink." She paused before zeroing in on what she saw as Sam's underlying problem. "What kind of a caseload are you carrying these days? Thirty-two, thirty-five hours a week?"

Sam nodded. It was the biggest caseload he had ever carried.

"On top of that you're teaching two mornings a week at Columbia Presbyterian. And on top of that you're working on an article for the *Journal of Psychiatry*." Her voice softened. "Sam, when a man's wife leaves after seven years of marriage . . ."

"Eight."

"Eight. When that happens, there's supposed to be some kind of emotional reaction. He is supposed to feel a lot of pain. He is supposed to feel a lot of anger. It's not particularly pleasant, but he's got to go through it. But—"

"But in my case," he interrupted again, wanting to provide the analysis before his mother did, "I am, number one, creating a highly elaborate system of highly structured activity that is specifically designed so that I can avoid dealing with my own emotions. And, number two, I am avoiding the possibility of any new emotional involvement, which I seem to find extremly threatening. Okay?"

Sam grinned—a student expecting praise from his teacher. In fact, the accuracy of his analysis caused him more pain. He was a good enough psychiatrist to recognize his own problem, but he could not seem to do anything about it.

"Please tell Uncle Charlie that I'm sorry I couldn't make it. And I'd like to take a rain check."

Grace knew when to stop pushing. "All right, all right," she said, coming toward him with outstretched arms. She gave him a hug and left the apartment without another word.

Beyond the window, the rain fell unceasingly. Sam stood in the center of his partially furnished living room, watching lightning flash over the darkened city.

4

Sam sat alone in the basement of the apartment building, waiting for his laundry to dry. The monotonous rumble of the electric drier did not disturb his reading. Spread on his lap was George Bynum's folder; he held a a half-empty can of Tab, which had turned warm in his hand. The clock on the wall had said 8:30 when he came down with his pillowcase stuffed with socks and underwear. Now it was almost ten.

The basement was a warren of storage lockers for the tenants, and rooms that held mysterious electrical and heating equipment looked after by Angelo, the superintendent. Sam had not seen him, although twice he thought he heard someone get off the elevator at the far end of the crooked corridor. It was crowded with bicycles and old trunks, with a damp, sweetish smell that Sam always associated with rats. Pools of light from the bare bulbs overhead stood at intervals along the corridor, empty and too far below the ground for the sounds of the storm to reach it.

Sam glanced in the direction of the drier. His laundry was probably done, but he was reluctant to leave. The basement provided an ideal place to read without interruption or distraction. He

turned a page and read his own entry for April 22:
"Bynum said he was in some kind of trouble at
the office . . ."

Sam thought he heard a footstep. He glanced
down the corridor; it was deserted as far as the first
turn. Someone brushed against a bicycle near the
elevator, and it crashed to the floor.

"Angelo?" Sam called, but there was no answer. Another tenant was probably hauling a bag
of dirty laundry off the elevator. Sam hoped he
wouldn't have to make conversation when the tenant came back to the washing machines.

Sam started to read again, but the light went out
in the corridor. He sat there for a long minute, staring at the darkness. Then he heard the sound
again.

"Angelo?"

The superintendent must have thrown the wrong
switch. Sam recognized his own wishful thinking;
something strange was going on. Vitucci's warning came back to him. The person who had killed
Bynum might also want to kill his psychiatrist, the
detective had said. He felt the force of that warning
for the first time and with it, the glimmerings of
fear.

Sam gathered his papers together and put them
inside the folder. He walked over to the drier and,
determined not to look over his shoulder, took his
laundry out and stuffed it into the pillowcase. He
would not give way to the irrational. The tension
he experienced went back to his childhood, a tension
between a terror of the unknown and the terror of
making a fool of himself.

He heard the sound again and wheeled around to

face the deserted corridor with the pool of darkness at the far end.

"Who's out there?" he demanded.

There was no answer and no other way out of the basement. Sam dropped a sock but was too distracted to pick it up. Carrying the pillowcase in one hand and the folder in the other, he started for the corridor.

"Who's there?" he repeated, urgently now. His heart pounded, feeding on the adenaline. Sam recognized all the symptoms of fear.

Holding the manilla folder and the bag of laundry in front of him, like a symbolic shield, he started down the corridor. The darkness beyond the turning was alleviated by the red glow of the light above the fire stairs. He could see the bicycle lying on its side. Nothing moved in the dimness.

He took a step in the direction of the elevator. A sudden hissing directly overhead flattened him against the wall. Directly above him, a broken pipe from the furnace shot steam into the air, dripping rusty water onto the concrete floor. Sam edged past the puddle, and noticed that the door leading to the stairs was open. It had been closed when he came down.

He started toward the elevator. It was darker there, with the open door behind him. He was almost running. He jabbed at the button, looking over his shoulder. A shriek sent a chill through his body. Something brushed against his foot, heavy and loathsome. He gasped, kicking out blindly. A rat disappeared into the gloom.

The elevator door had opened. Sam turned to

see the dark silhouette of a woman beside him, her face hidden in shadow. For an instant, as the woman stared, Sam imagined the death of Bynum —the up-raised arm, the gleam of the knife blade. Then she backed up, into the light; it was Brooke Reynolds.

"Doctor Rice?" she said.

He stepped quickly into the elevator and pushed the button. He tried to control his breathing, staring into the darkness.

"You frightened me," Brooke said. "What happened to the lights?"

"I don't know. Somebody must have pulled the wrong switch." He was surprised to see her, both glad and suspicious.

"Are you all right?" She seemed genuinely concerned.

"Fine, I'm fine." It was not a very convincing performance, Sam knew. "Well . . . hello."

He wanted to ask what the hell she was doing in his apartment building late at night. But she took a package from beneath her arm and offered it to him. Sam regarded her warily. She wore the same tailored coat; her soft blond hair had been freshly brushed. Her smile was irresistible.

"Here," she said, forcing the package on him, "this is for you." She laughed at his confusion. "I felt so badly about that figurine I broke in your office."

So it was a present. "Miss Reynolds, you didn't have to do that."

"I don't even know if you'll like it." The element of uncertainty was one of the most charming things about her, Sam decided. He tried to hand the present back.

"This really isn't necessary."

"Please."

The elevators doors opened on Sam's floor.

"Thank you," he said, "thank you very much. That's very sweet of you."

"You know, you shouldn't leave your apartment door open. Anybody could walk in."

She must have tried his apartment first and then gone looking for him. It occurred to Sam that the person who turned off the lights in the basement could be waiting in his half-furnished living room. He could be waiting just inside the door.

"Well," said Brooke, "it's late, and I have to go. I'm sorry if I disturbed you."

"Why don't you come in for a drink?" If Sam was to be murdered, at least he could provide a witness.

"No, I can't."

"Please." He took her arm and added truthfully, "It would make me feel a lot better if you did."

Sam escorted Brooke down the hall, hugging his laundry, his notes on George Bynum's analysis that contained intimate descriptions of Brooke, and the package she had given him. Sam had once vowed that he would never allow himself to become involved in the life of a patient, as his mother had become involved so often. Now Sam was intimately involved in a patient's death.

He entered the apartment ahead of her, talking loudly. "Some lights," he said, switching them on. With a sigh he noted that the foyer and the living room were empty. "Come in, please. Here let me take that."

He dumped his things on the table and helped her off with her coat. He remembered her perfume from that afternoon. She had clear, almost transluscent skin, like a child's, and a slender waist. Her breasts, however, were definitely not those of a child. Sam felt a stab of desire—he had not made love to a woman in more than a month.

"The living room is right here," he said, first pushing open the door of the kitchen to make sure it was empty. He turned on the lamp next to the wing chair, abolishing the shadows in the room. "Sit down, make yourself comfortable."

Brooke seemed uneasy. She sat on the edge of the chair and looked around.

"Did you just move in?" she asked.

"No, someone moved out. I guess I should get some more furniture." He had to check the rest of the apartment. "Excuse me, I'll be right back."

He walked down the hall and turned on the light in the bedroom, the one Sarah had used during their last year together, when they were trying to resolve their differences. *Her* differences, Sam thought. The room was empty except for the cardboard boxes, an old vacuum cleaner, and Sam's Fugi bicycle. Sarah had taken the bed, the one made of curly maple, with a canopy, that they had bought together on a weekend trip to Vermont.

He opened the closet door. His summer clothes hung there, together with a few outdated dresses that Sarah had left behind. They had a sad, musty smell, like something lost and forgotten.

"All right," he said to himself, "I know there's

no one here." But the irrational fear stayed with him. He lived in a secure building, yet the doorman had let Brooke in without asking Sam's permission. Maybe someone who was not as pretty as she, and a lot more dangerous, could also get past him.

"Doctor Rice," she called out to him, "are you okay?"

He wondered if she had heard him talking to himself—the crazy psychiatrist. "I'm fine, I'm fine."

He went into the bathroom, turned on the light, and swept the shower curtain inside. Empty. He checked his bedroom and closet without result.

"Doctor Rice, if this is a bad time . . ."

"No, no," he said. "This is a good, a really *good* time."

He opened the hall closet, the last potential hiding place. It was empty, too. Relieved, he decided not to deprive Angelo and the doorman of their Christmas tips, after all.

"Classic childhood fear of the dark," he said, returning to the living room. "Oh, yes, I offered you a drink."

That room was also empty. He stared at the wing chair where Brooke had been, then turned around, almost colliding with her. He grabbed her arms, steadying them both, and Brooke began to laugh.

"I don't have anything to drink," he admitted.

"That's all right."

"What about club soda?"

"Yes." She nodded, as if club soda was a wonderful idea.

"Grapefruit juice," Sam said, remembering he had some. Anything was better than club soda, for

39

such a beautiful and unexpected visitor. He was acutely aware of how close she stood to him.

"Fine," said Brooke, watching him.

"Tea!" Now there was an inspiration. "How about some tea?"

"Tea would be very nice."

"The kitchen's in here."

He led her back, in a dreamy state that was half, relief, half infatuation. It had been a while since Sam had had company—other than his mother—and he hadn't realized how much he missed talking to someone outside of a session.

Sam put the kettle on the stove. Brooke inspected his cooking utensils, which he rarely used nowadays, and the collection of cookbooks. She drifted into the dining room.

"I was worried about you this morning," he admitted, taking a canister of Earl Grey out of the cupboard. "You seemed very upset."

"Shhhh."

Sam froze. "What is it?"

Brooke didn't answer. He followed her into the dining room, where she stood before the window, looking out.

"I love the sound of rain," she said. "When I lived in Florence with my father, we had a house in Fiesole. My room was on the top floor. I used to love to lie there at night and listen to the sound of the rain."

"When did you live in Florence?"

"Ten years ago. But I'm sure George told you all about . . ."

She broke off, as if Sam already knew so much about her that she could tell him nothing new. The assumption offended him, as if he were a doctor and nothing else.

"What?" he said bluntly. "What did he tell me?"

They were both surprised by the vehemence in Sam's voice. Brooke assumed she was trespassing in the forbidden territory of a patient's secrets.

"I'm sorry."

But Sam wouldn't let it pass. "What did George tell me about you?"

"I don't understand . . ."

"What does it matter what he told me about you?" Sam was more than capable of forming his own, independent opinion of her, and he wanted her to know it.

Brooke smiled as the realization dawned on her. She walked into the living room and brought back the box.

"Here, I wanted to show you this."

They stood very close to one another. She opened the box and carefully lifted out a statuette that was clearly not an imitation, a Greek woman with delicate arms and a face of classic beauty. The value of the gift, and the thought behind it, stunned Sam.

"I hope you like it." She pressed the statue on him. "She's a Tanagra figure from the fourth century B.C. I love her. I think she's very beautiful." Brooke swept the hair from her own face, transported by the presence of work of votive art. "These were placed in tombs to protect the spirits of the dead from . . ." And she laughed, "from clumsy people like me probably. Do you like it?"

"Yes, I do." It was an understatement. Sam wanted to say much more, but he was out of practice. "I returned the watch to Mrs. Bynum's lawyer. I didn't mention you."

Brooke's gratitude was apparent. They stood admiring the statue in silence, uncertain of their own and each other's motions.

Finally she said, "It's very late. I should be going."

Sam followed her into the hall. She slipped into her coat and put her hand on the doorknob.

"Wait a minute . . ." he began. He wanted her to stay, but he couldn't bring himself to ask her. And Brooke wasn't going to say it for him.

"Thank you," she said, smiling and pulling up the collar against her cheeks.

"Thank you"—he held up the Tanagra figurine and added—"for her."

5

"Well, I'm afraid I've really done it this time."
George Bynum's voice had lost none of its playfulness. The words, spoken a few days before his death and preserved on tape, reminded Sam of the fragility of human life. He had come to the office early after a restless night, hoping to gain from the tapes some insight into the events that had suddenly overtaken his life. He was interested in seeing justice done, but he was also intrigued with Brooke Reynolds and her role in the affair.

Sam took a sip of hot coffee from the Styrofoam cup and hit the "play" button again on the console. ". . . my assistant quit," Bynam was saying, "and I had sort of promised the job to one of the girls I work with. I mean, we've been . . . you know . . ."

Bynum had had difficulty coming right out and saying the word *sex*. This was strange, since he engaged in so much of it, without apparent remorse. Sam remembered him sitting in the chair across from Sam's desk, smoking Gauloises, perfectly at ease, an adolescent smile on his full lips. Sam knew that beneath that smooth exterior lay anxieties of considerable strength and complexity.

"Anyway, yesterday afternoon this woman came walking into the office. I don't know why, but before I knew what happened, I gave her the job. Her name is Brooke Reynolds, and she's very shy, very subdued." There was a long pause while Bynum took a drag on his cigarette. Then he had said, grinning, "I really am in a lot of trouble."

Sam consulted his own notes taken on that day: "This is the first time since Bynum started analysis that he has mentioned a women by name. Either he's getting better, or it's the girl. I'm betting on the girl."

Brooke had been good for Bynum, there was no doubt about that. Sam wasn't so sure that Bynum was good for her, however. He advanced the tape to the next session.

". . . the more I see of the new girl in the office, the more I think she's definitely your type. . . . You know, there's something about Brooke that's very endearing. Last night I was walking her home, and I asked her if she had a boyfriend. She got very red in the face and said No. . . . Actually, I think she has a crush on me. I thought I might give her a try. But the more I think about it, the more I think the two of you would be perfect together. I'm not kidding, Doctor. I can tell she would really go for you. . . . It's too bad, really."

Sam shut off the machine and sat for a moment staring at the building across the street. Secretaries were arriving for work; the business day had begun. Sam had work to do himself, and patients to see, but he could not get Brooke out of his mind. Bynum's words made him uneasy, as if the dead man had been blessed with omniscience. Too bad he couldn't have foreseen his own death, Sam thought. But maybe Bynum had foreseen it.

He turned on the tape machine again, picking up the next session he had conducted with Bynum.

"What would you say if I told you I had been to bed with your girlfriend?" Bynum asked, and Sam felt his discomfort grow. Was it possible to be jealous of a murdered patient?

"Aren't you curious?"

Bynum had paused, waiting for Sam's reaction, and then said, "What the hell, it's my seventy-five dollars! Crispin's is handling the Maddow estate. He's the big collector of antiquities, mostly archaic Greek and Coptic. But then you're not interested in that, Doctor. There's a lot of cataloguing to the done. Night before last, Brooke and I worked late. Everyone else had gone home, and—I really don't know why; I guess I just wanted to see what would happen—I reached across and put my hand on the back of her neck. . . . She didn't move. She didn't do anything; she didn't say a word. It was very quiet; all I could hear was her breathing. I moved my hand down her back. . . . I remember I was surprised that she wasn't wearing a bra. The whole time my mind was very clear, very sharp. I kept thinking, I could stop this now. I mean, I could have passed this off as, I don't know, as some kind of affectionate gesture. But I reached over and kissed her."

There was a pause while Bynum lit another cigarette. Sam heard him exhale; Bynum had enjoyed telling the story. He seemed to care more for Brooke than for the others.

"At first she didn't respond. I mean, there was nothing. And I thought, Oh, God. I've really done it, I'm in trouble. But then she kissed back, and

I held her. . . . You know that incredible smell women have back behind the ear, and along the neck? It's like . . . it's like . . ."

Here Sam remembered Bynum's hand shaking as he smoked. Was he affected by the erotic details of his own story, or was he afraid of something?

". . . and then I unbuttoned her blouse, and I put my hand on her breast. She didn't make any move to stop me, but I could feel her heart beating, she was so scared. . . . Am I boring you?"

Bynum had cancelled the next two sessions. He told Sam only that he was going away with a girlfriend. The next time he came to Sam's office, he looked haggard and smoked more heavily. *"God,"* he had told Sam, *"she is extraordinary."* Bynum was enthralled with the way Brooke kissed, her fondness for it, and how kissing turned her on.

"You haven't asked me about Brooke," Bynum had said. "Aren't you curious about her?"

"Should I be?" asked Sam.

"Sure. Here, I took a photograph of her."

It was still clipped to Bynum's folder. Sam had not been as impressed with Brooke when he had seen the photograph as he was when she walked into his office. He had thought at first that she was simply pretty. Bynum's opinion of her had interested him more, and the way the patient wanted Sam to like her. Women sometimes fell in love with their analysts, while men often wanted to make their analysts happy. Bynum had reached that stage in his analysis where he was dependent on his doctor. And Sam had been unable to really help him.

He pressed the play button again.

"Come to think of it, Doctor, you never ask about Brooke. You ask about my wife, you ask about my boss, but you don't ask about Brooke. . . . Why is that? You know, I think you're beginning to have a problem about her. . . . No, no, I'm serious. I really mean it. . . . You poor guy, you're crazier than I am."

Bynum had become annoyed because Sam didn't show more interest. The irony was that Sam had finally developed a problem with Brooke, as his patient put it. But Sam's problem was not nearly as great as Bynum's, which had proved terminal. Sam was determined to find out what that problem was.

He advanced the tape to the following session, the next to last one. Bynum had seemed more nervous than ever, and depressed. After half an hour of questioning, he had asked, "What would you say about somebody who—I'm just talking hypothetically now—somebody who you found out had actually killed somebody? And let's say that, because it happened in Italy and because her family was rich, nobody ever found out. . . . Actually, I'm the only person who knows about it, except for you. Anyway, what I'm trying to say is this: If somebody had done that before—killed someone—is it likely that they will do it again?"

It was something that had nagged at Sam since the night before. Brooke had mentioned Florence while at his apartment; it was only later that he remembered Bynum's reference to Italy.

Sam spun the tape to the final session with Bynum. He remembered that it had been briefer— and desperate. Listening to it again, Sam was struck by the distance in Bynum's voice. No more jokes about Brooke and the doctor, no more sexy descriptions of the time spent with her. Bynum had receded from the grasp of his psychiatrist; he was in retreat. It reminded Sam of their first session together, without trust or intimacy.

"Oh, listen, Doctor," Bynum said at the end of the tape. Sam remembered that he had been standing in the middle of the office, putting his cigarettes away, and the recorder was still running. "All that morbid junk I told you last week, about someone who had killed someone else. I wish you would forget about it, okay? What I mean is . . . I was mistaken."

What had he been mistaken about? The killing? Or was it a mistake to have told Sam about it? Was he talking about Brooke, or someone else?

Sam rewound the tape, took it off the machine and replaced it in the plastic cassette carrier marked *Bynum, G.* Instead of returning the tape to the library, he pulled out a desk drawer and hid it under the Manhattan telephone directory.

His coffee was stone cold. The sun had climbed into the autumn sky, drying the streets and filling his office with the glow of Chablis. He thought about the final session and Bynum's dream. The patient was in retreat, all right, but his description of the dream was detailed and frightening, even to a professional. Now Sam carefully reconstructed it.

In the dream, Bynum had arrived in his own car at a strange and beautiful country house. It was dusk. He left the car in the gravel drive and walked beneath a trellis heavy with a flowering vine. The house had French doors and weathered cedar shakes like the siding on beach homes, and it nestled into the hillside. The attached greenhouse brimmed with huge, broad-leafed plants. The setting was beautifully landscaped, and the carved eaves of the sloping room had been painted with flowers. But there was something morbid about the place. Bynum saw a white cat crouched on the peak of the roof, its paws drawn under, staring at him.

A brass bell hung next to the door, green with age. It rang sonorously as Bynum touched it with his elbow. At that moment he looked through the jungle of domesticated plants, at a small girl on the far side of the French door. Her white gown seemed to glow in the half-light; her flaxen hair was brushed smooth. The girl disturbed Bynum, but he walked toward her and found himself in an empty living room. A fire burned in the grate. The furniture was tasteful and sumptuous. An exquisite black lacquer cabinet stood against one wall, highlighted with gilt scroll work.

Bynum was drawn to the cabinet. He raised a hand to open it, and a shriek made him cower. He looked up at a fierce, gap-beaked eagle perched on the cabinet. It screamed, lurched at him again, and then settled back to watch.

Cautiously, Bynum opened the lacquered cabinet. Inside, he found a small green box. He did not open it, but guiltily slipped the box into his pocket. He turned around and saw the little girl again, sitting in an upholstered chair, holding a stuffed bear. She stared at him, an enigmatic smile on her lips. Then with a casual, chilling gesture she grasped one of the bear's button eyes and pulled it out.

Blood appeared where the eye had been. It ran down the bear's face and dripped onto the girl's thigh, and from there it dripped to the floor. Dark and viscous, the blood would not stop flowing. Gradually it spread over the floor, one long rivulet extending in Bynum's direction. He felt a growing sense of terror as the blood approached, yet he could not move his feet.

The girl stood, still smiling, and waded toward him, through the blood. Bynum forced himself to flee. A door opened miraculously in the corner, leading to a corridor, and he followed it. The girl pursued him, expressionless now, methodical. Though Bynum was running, he couldn't lose her.

He passed through another room. The French doors led to a patio, but Bynum could not get them open. Frantically, he rattled the handles. He ran to the foot of a staircase that led steeply upward to a sharp turn. The girl was no longer behind him, and he started up the stairs, clinging to a thin, wooden rail. At the turning he looked back, and she was there again. Slowly, she mounted the stairs after him.

Bynum opened the door at the top and entered a bedroom. An oval mirror stood against one wall; in it he could see the stairs, but the girl did not reappear. Bynum took the green box from his jacket pocket. It had diminished in size, and it fell from his hand and tumbled on the rug.

At that moment a blast of wind threw open glass doors leading to a balcony. The girl stood in the eerie half-light, arms outstretched, her diaphanous gown raked by leaves carried by the gale. She had grown to huge proportions. Her hair lashed her face; her fingers curled into claws. Where her eyes had been, lifeless holes gaped at him.

Bynum heard the eagle's shrieking; it was his own screams.

The telephone on Sam's desk was ringing.

6

Sam paid the cabbie and stepped out onto the pavement of East Seventy-ninth Street. He looked up at the gilt-edged windows and the dark marble facade of Crispin's, the oldest auction house in New York. The ultimate meeting place of culture and money, Crispin's seemed the least likely establishment to be involved in a murder. Crispin's was known for the unprecedented prices paid for works of art, and for the attendance of films stars and European nobility, and not for the tawdry elements of human passion. Much of the publicity caused by Bynum's murder could be attributed to the place. The press loved dealing with Crispin's.

The uniformed guard in the foyer directed Sam to the third floor, where Detective Vitucci was taking statements from Crispin's employees. He had uncovered some information that he wanted Sam to clarify, although he would not say over the telephone what that information might be.

The elevator's polished mahogany panelling reflected Sam's image; he looked tired and on edge. He adjusted his tie and walked out into the bustling reception area. An attractive middle-aged woman sat at a Louis XV desk, selling catalogues of the upcoming auction to clients who had the well-bred air of collectors and art *amateurs*. The opulence of Crispin's had a soothing effect on Sam: it was hard to imagine George Bynum working there, but then Bynum's exterior had been as smooth as his inner life was tumultuous.

There was no sign of Brooke. Through tall double doors he could see the auction room, with comfortable chairs arranged in rows facing the ornate lectern, and a low stage for displaying works of art. The inlaid ceiling and travertine columns reminded Sam of a Venetian palace. Heavy brocade curtains covered the windows.

Sam asked the receptionist where he could find Detective Joseph Vitucci. "Just a moment," she said pleasantly, although her smile lost some of its professional charm. She picked up the telephone, murmured a few words into it, and told Sam that someone would be with him shortly.

He took up a position between an armoire and a china cabinet, out of the flow of traffic. After a few minutes, the elevator doors opened and a young woman with auburn hair stepped off, a sheaf of papers under one arm. Conservatively dressed in pleated skirt, sweater, and circle pin at the collar, she reminded Sam of a cheerleader on her way to class, with a strong stride and an open, pretty face.

"Doctor Rice?"

"Yes."

"Hi. I'm Gail Phillips. Just a moment, and I'll be right with you." She picked up the phone on the receptionist's desk and began to talk to a client. Her manner was friendly, direct, efficient—an obvious asset in a place like Crispin's.

She hung up. "Sorry to keep you waiting. Brooke

asked me to take care of you. I was one of George
Bynum's assistants."

They shook hands. Gail seemed the antithesis of
Brooke, who was soft and enigmatic.

"Have you ever been to Crispin's before?" Gail
asked.

"No, I haven't."

"Shall I give you a tour on the way up? It's a
long walk."

"Why not?"

She laughed, the light-hearted tour guide, and led
him into the long, airy hallway. "Crispin's is the
oldest auction house in the United States. It was
founded in 1811 and has been operating without
interruption ever since. In there is the auction
room."

They passed behind the empty chairs and into a
gallery full of oil paintings in bright, warm colors.
Sam was amazed to see a Cezanne and two Gaugans
sitting side by side on sturdy easels. Two uniformed
guards stood in the corner, bored with their jobs,
wearing guns and beepers.

"In this gallery are the Impressionist and Post-
Impressionist paintings that go up for sale tomorrow night. Now, when something gets turned over
to Crispin's for sale—like the Maddow estate, for
instance, a very important antiquities collection
that's worth over fifty million dollars and will go
on sale soon—every single object has to be num-
bered, and a file card made for it . . ."

They passed through a room full of eighteenth-
and nineteenth-century American furniture. Sam
expected to see Brooke at any moment.

"And after that it has to be checked for authenticity. Because if we sell something as authentic, then we're responsible for it if it turns out to be a fraud. Are you sure you're up to all this?"

"I am if you are," Sam said. He was actually enjoying the tour.

"In here, we have an exhibition of early American paintings and furniture. They'll be auctioned off next week. Crispin's has branches in Paris, London, Geneva, Boston, and Los Angeles. We have an excellent Blue Cross program," she continued, "which includes psychiatric benefits. But I'm sure you're aware of that."

Sam couldn't tell if she was joking. She opened a heavy metal door, and they entered the stairwell. "Downstairs are all the public rooms—more exhibition and auction rooms, and so on." They climbed to the next floor. "Up here is where all the slave labor takes place."

She led him into a cavernous hall full of furniture, paintings, art objects, and what looked like plain junk. Wooden crates were stacked to the ceiling against the far wall; packing, boards, and rope littered the floor. Men in coveralls hustled back and forth between the piles of merchandise and the island in the center of the room—a vast table where two men in their shirt-sleeves were unpacking the individual pieces.

"Good lord," said Sam. Crispin's reminded him of a cultured, urbane person whose mind was really full of chaos, crowded with all the bits and pieces of a past life.

"Some mess, isn't it?" Gail said. "But it all gets sorted out eventually."

They almost collided with a man carrying a crystal chandelier.

"Where does it all come from?" Sam asked.

"Estates, galleries, private collections, but mostly from ordinary people all over the country. Whenever anything comes to Crispin's, it's receipted and sent to the proper department for cataloguing. Sculpture to the sculpture department, prints to the print department—" they passed two enameled elephants still in crates; they were the color of limes —"green elephants to the green elephant department," said Gail. "Just kidding."

They entered another room, smaller but just as crowded. The merchandise was obviously finer and more expensive.

"This is the storage area for the Oriental department. Once an object has been authenticated, a form is filled out and the object is sent to be photographed. We have our own photographers here. Then groups of similar objects are put together for auction. At that point, people in the department spread out the photographs and put them in order of sale, and they're sent to the printer."

At last they entered the suite of offices. Sam was thoroughly disoriented; he could not have found his way back to the reception area unaided. He noticed that the door at the end of the hall was marked ANTIQUITIES.

"About a week before the auction," Gail was saying, determined to finish her spiel, "everything is taken downstairs and put on exhibition, and the night before, they are taken backstage. Finally, on the day of the sale, they are brought out and hopefully sold."

Vitucci emerged from one of the offices. He wore his police issue vest under his jacket and the uncertain expression of someone in a foreign country. Sam guessed that the investigation was not going too well.

"That's the end of the speech," Gail said, "and the end of the tour, and"—she laughed, making a bow—"here's the police!"

"Thank you very much."

"You're welcome." She went swinging down the hall.

"Doctor," said Vitucci, as if he had recognized an old friend, "I appreciate your coming over. I know you're a busy man. I'll try not to keep you too long."

Sam followed him into the office, a luxurious glass cubicle with a leather-top desk, an ornate lamp, and a stack of books about Greek antiquities.

"No problem," said Sam, realizing that the office had been George Bynum's. He and Vitucci settled into upholstered chairs. It reflected Bynum's sense of style.

Vitucci picked up the phone and punched a button without success. He hung up, leaned far to one side so he could see down the hall, and called out, "Oh, Miss Wilson, could you come in now?"

Miss Wilson was a stunning brunette in her early twenties. Whoever did the hiring at Crispin's, Sam thought, liked beautiful women. This one was obviously less than pleased to be at the beck and call of a policeman.

"Thanks," said Vitucci, only dimly aware of Miss Wilson's displeasure. Then he turned to Sam. "Yesterday when we were talking, you said the deceased came to see you twice a week, is that right?"

Sam nodded, and Vitucci opened the appointments book given to him by the secretary.

"According to this, George Bynum was seeing you five times a week."

"That's impossible," said Sam.

Vitucci looked up at Miss Wilson. "How often did Mr. Bynum have an appointment with his psychiatrist?"

"Five times a week."

"Are you sure?" asked Sam. He could easily imagine what Bynum did on those days he was supposed to have been with Sam.

"Of course I'm sure." Miss Wilson sounded insulted. "Now, if that's all, I have a lot of work to do."

"That's fine," Vitucci said. "Thank you. And would you close the door, please?"

She pulled the door closed behind her. Vitucci lowered his voice, anyway. "We found out that George Bynum was fooling around with at least one of the girls here at Crispin's."

"And you're going to ask me who that is," said Sam.

"And you're gonna say that's confidential information."

Sam nodded. They had already been through that.

"Now, look, Doctor. I found out a couple of more things since I talked to you last. One, we're pretty sure that George Bynum was killed by a women. Two, his wife was in Florida; we know it wasn't her. The psych guys at Forensic drew up a kind of psychological portrait of the killer, and they think she'll try again. Now I don't want to crowd you about this, but I get the feeling you know a lot more than you're telling me."

Sam felt a chill, a kind of inner horror. He had little faith in the police's psychological profile, but there was a chance they were right.

"Just because George Bynum may have been a son of a bitch," Vitucci was saying, "is no reason for you not to help."

The criticism touched a raw nerve. Bynum was a son of a bitch, Sam had to admit. His teasing Sam about Brooke, her beauty, and how she would have liked Sam, had she met him, was not an attempt to flatter him, but a sadistic goading. Bynum had taken advantage of people all around him. But he was still a human being. At least he had been.

"Wait a minute," Sam said. "George Bynum was a patient of mine." He wondered if Vitucci knew what that entailed. "I'm as much concerned about what happened to him as you are."

The detective was clearly not impressed.

"Doctor Rice, I don't know what they can do to a psychiatrist who withholds information"—the implication was that Vitucci would find out. "—but I can promise you this for a fact: you're gonna end up in a lot of trouble."

Sam got up and walked out of the office.

"If you don't get yourself killed first," Vitucci called after him. "Thanks for coming over."

Sam almost collided with Brooke, who had come out of the Antiquities office carrying a sheaf of papers. Sam's suspicions about her slipped away.

"Oh, hello," he said.

Brooke stared at him as if he were a total

stranger. With a glance in at Vitucci, who was watching, she stepped around Sam and hurried down the hall, her hips moving provocatively beneath the full, pleated skirt.

Gail, up to her elbows in the filing cabinet, had also seen the encounter.

"Nice try," she said jokingly.

Sam stood on the pavement outside Crispin's, lost in thought. He had expected Brooke to be waiting there with some explanation for her behavior. She had no logical reason to be afraid of the police, or so it seemed to him. But Sam's own reasoning had become affected by the sheer magnetic attraction of Brooke Reynolds. He needed professional help and someone he could trust.

He stepped into a telephone booth, fishing some coins out of his pocket, and dialed his mother's number.

The phone rang once and Grace Rice answered, "Yes?"

"Hi, Mom. It's Sam."

"Hi. How are you?" She sounded surprised.

"Fine," he said. "Listen, I got to thinking, why don't we have dinner tonight? Just the two of us." He tried to sound casual. "I'll order some Chinese, and—"

"All right, Sam," Grace interrupted. "What's up?"

He had never been able to put anything over on Grace.

"Well," Sam admitted, "as a matter of fact, I've got a little problem."

"Personal or professional?"

"Professional."

There was a long pause. "I've got a group until nine," she said finally. "I'll be there as soon after that as I can."

"Thank you."

"See you then."

Relieved, Sam hung up. Sometimes it was wonderful to have a mother who was also a psychiatrist.

7

Sam cancelled all his afternoon sessions, something he had never done before. He put George Bynum's case folder, his own notes, and the tapes in his briefcase and he left the building by the side door. Vitucci's warning came back to Sam again and again. He did not consider himself a particularly brave man, but Sam was not going to be frightened into telling the police what he knew about Brooke. At least not until he had formed a theory himself.

Objectively, the implications that Brooke was involved in Bynum's murder were very strong. Her suspicious behavior did not help that impression. But Sam had been trained as a psychiatrist to deal with subjective phenomena, to search for contradictory meaning in a person's words and behavior, to free the soul from its empirical strait jacket. His instincts told him that Brooke was not a criminal and not psychotic, but troubled by some experience in her past.

The doorman outside his apartment building tipped his hat as Sam entered. Sam started to ask him if he had had any mysterious visitors or enquiries, but checked himself; the man would think Sam paranoid. He rode up alone in the elevator and let himself into the silence of his home, full of the slanting rays of the afternoon sun.

Moving quickly and with determination, Sam set up a blackboard in the living room, spread his materials on the desk, and began to replay Bynum's tapes, searching for anything he might have missed before. He chalked bits of pertinent information on the board, as reminders to himself. He wrote in Vitucci's information: where the body was found, the excessive number of wounds, the official theory that the murderer was a woman, and that she would strike again. He drew a diagram of Bynum's life as Sam knew it—Crispin's, home, and the love affairs.

Then he made a list of suspects. In addition to Brooke, he wrote down the name of Bynum's wife, who could possibly have had her husband killed while she was in Florida. He added the names of the other two young women who worked with Bynum, Gail Phillips and the secretary, Miss Wilson, who had shown hostility toward Vitucci and Sam. There were plenty of other women at Crispin's who could have been involved with Bynum; he wrote the letter X at the bottom of the list, signifying the unknown.

It was dark outside when he finished. He sat back and studied the board, vaguely aware of the sounds of evening traffic many stories below. The most prominent name on the board was Brooke's, appearing in more categories than any other. Sam realized that he was no closer to a solution than when he had begun.

The doorbell rang. Expecting Grace Rice, Sam hurried through the dark hallway and opened the door. The woman standing there was not his mother, however.

"Brooke!"

She was *extra*-ordinarily beautiful as well as upset. There was an air of innocence, even vulnerability, about her that made Sam momentarily ashamed of himself for having suspected her at all.

"What's the matter?" he asked.

"What did you tell the police about me?"

Without waiting for an answer, she brushed past him, into the apartment. Her cheeks were flushed; her eyes darted about the apartment, as if she expected to find Vitucci there, in the shadows.

"Nothing," Sam said. "I didn't tell them anything."

"Don't lie to me."

"*Lie* to you? Sam felt a surge of anger; he had done everything he could to avoid telling the police about her.

"Please," she said, her voice growing small. "I hate that. I hate it when people lie to me. I really thought I could trust you."

"Brooke, I didn't tell the police anything about you. Now what's going on?"

"You must have told them something." She had opened her purse, and now she pulled out an empty packet of Gauloises. Sam had never seen her so agitated. "That policeman had me in his office all afternoon. You must have told them something about George and me. You're the only one who knew about us."

"Brooke, listen to me." Sam took her arm and led her into the living room. "They're going to have to question everyone who knew George Bynum. They seem to think that Bynum was killed by a woman."

She looked up at him, stunned. She reminded Sam of a little girl at that moment, lost and without much hope of being found.

"That's not possible," she said.

He wanted to ask her why, but he added, "I guess they found some evidence."

"Did they tell you what it was?"

"No. But they also know that George was having an affair."

"All I've asked," Brooke said miserably, "is to be left out of this, and nobody's listening to me."

"Wait a minute." He took her by the shoulders, without trying to hide his anger. "You were having an affair with him; you were sleeping with him. You're going to have to tell them what was going on. Tell them about all those evenings you worked late together—they'll listen to that."

It was the first time he had allowed himself to make a moral judgment, and it surprised him. He released Brooke, and she turned away.

"But you don't understand."

"What?" he challenged. "What don't I understand?"

"One night we were working very late. Everyone else had gone home. I didn't think anything about it, and then all of a sudden I realized that George was standing next to me, very close. I knew something was going to happen. He touched me, he kissed me . . ." She seemed to shudder. "He seemed very sure of himself. We made love that night. It should never have happened. I hadn't been involved with anyone for a very long time, I knew from the start that it was a terrible mistake."

Sam thought of Bynum's description of that evening, the way he had cupped Brooke's breast in his hand, the eager, almost animalistic quality of her kisses. She seemed an entirely different person now.

"I kept trying to break it off," she said. "Friday night—the night he was killed—I was with him, and I told him I wanted to end it. But he kept . . . pushing. That was the last time I saw him. You see, it was just because I was so lonely. It was stupid of me, I know. You have to believe me."

She turned back to him, and he saw that she was in pain.

"I never, never loved him," she added.

Sam felt a great sense of relief. "All right," he said, trying to comfort Brooke. "Then what are you so frightened of?"

Brooke gestured helplessly, as if she wanted to tell him, but could not. She asked, "You don't think I did it—killed him—do you?"

"No," he said, with as much conviction as he could muster.

She gazed past him, toward the blackboard. It was angled so she could not read the writing.

"Oh, I didn't know you were working. I'm sorry."

"It's not important," Sam told her.

"What is it?"

She started to walk around the blackboard. On impulse, Sam grasped her arm and pulled her toward him. She didn't resist, her hands sliding up his arms, her body softly meeting his. Before Sam knew it, he was kissing her, a sensation that went beyond anything he had previously imagined. Brooke was warm, and open to him, yet somehow saddened. She seemed to have longed for this, and to have dreaded it at the same time. All the passion that he had denied since his wife left him threatened to erupt. After the first kiss, he moved his hands down past the small of her back and over her hips, thrusting against her. Together they moved in simulation of the act of love. Sam knew that he had to exercise some control, that they had entered a dangerous place together. But Brooke would not release him. The kissing seemed to transform her. She slipped her hands behind his neck, her tongue touching him, moaning.

They pulled apart, regarding one another with surprise. Then Brooke kissed him again. The sound of the doorbell ripped them apart, a violent intrusion that left them both stunned and disoriented.

"It's my mother," Sam said, in answer to Brooke's unspoken question.

Slowly she returned to reality. "I have to go anyway."

They walked to the door. Sam put his hands in his pockets to hide their shaking.

"I'll call you."

"That's okay." Brooke smiled distractedly.

Sam opened the door.

"Sorry I'm late," began Grace, already slipping out of her coat, "but traffic was really terrible—"

The expression on Grace's face when she saw Brooke was worth all the trouble and worry Sam had undergone since Bynum had been killed: for once his mother was speechless.

"I'd like for you to meet Brooke Reynolds," Sam said. "Brooke, this is my mother."

Beneath Grace Rice's surprise lay admiration

and approval. She obviously liked the looks of Sam's visitor.

"How do you do?" she asked Brooke, and then turned to Sam. "If this is inconvenient, I'll—"

"No, no," Brooke said quickly, "I was just leaving."

She stepped past Grace and walked toward the elevator; the intimacy and the apparent trust that Sam had felt a few moments before had disappeared.

"I've got an appointment," Brooke added. "Very nice to meet you."

"Wait a minute," Sam said, disappointed and slightly annoyed. "I'll get you a taxi."

"No, please." The desperation had returned to her voice. "It isn't necessary."

Brooke smiled bravely and jabbed at the button for the elevator; the doors opened.

"Sam," Grace said, "I can come back later . . ."

"I'll just get her a cab."

The elevator doors were already closing. The last thing Sam saw of Brooke was the dark slash of her coat and her wide, incredibly blue eyes.

"Good lord," said Grace, and Sam couldn't mistake the wry quality in her voice. "Whatever I did wrong, I'm sorry."

She assumed that Sam had a lover. This time he wished she was right.

8

Brooke asked the doorman to get her a cab. She tipped him and settled back against the worn upholstery, trying to regain some composure. The cab sped along Central Park West, and she could see the hundreds of white lights outlining the trees around Tavern on the Green, and the waning autumn moon east of the city. They drove toward it, along the winding black ribbon of road that split the park and delivered her safely to the well-swept pavement of East Eighty-first Street. She lived equally close to the Metropolitan Museum of Art and Crispin's; one of those institutions threatened to be her undoing.

She glanced at her watch as she stepped out of the cab: she was on time. She really did have an appointment, although Sam Rice clearly had not believed her. Whatever else Brooke was, she was not a liar. One reason she feared the police was her own sometimes uncontrollable desire to tell about her past. Too much truth, Brooke thought, was not in anyone's interest.

Brooke rode the elevator to the third floor. An Oriental man stood waiting in the hallway, a briefcase in his hand. He wore a black overcoat and seemed prepared to remain there forever.

"Oh, Mr. Chong," said Brooke, "I'm sorry. I didn't realize I was late."

"You not late," he said. "Me two minutes early. Good evening."

"Good evening, Mr. Chong."

They shook hands, as they always did. Chong had a tight smile and powerful hands. She let him into her apartment, a spacious Victorian efficiency with twelve-foot ceilings and heavy moldings. Brooke had chose it for the atmosphere and the faded elegance: dark panelling and old casement windows. She had chosen furniture to match— heavy-lacquered period pieces and over-stuffed chairs. The statue of Pallas Athena, which she had bought from Crispin's herself, seemed airy, almost weightless on its pedestal in the corner of the living room.

On clear days Brooke liked to throw back the drapes and let the sun into her world. But now the drapes were drawn, and the lamps threw long shadows across the Oriental carpet.

Chong sat down to wait, very proper, his hands folded in his lap. Brooke excused herself and went into the bedroom. Without hesitation she began to undress—first the skirt, then the silk blouse. Soon she stood naked before the vanity. She allowed her eyes to briefly tarry on the fullness of her breasts, her narrow waist, and softly rounded hips. The memory of Sam's kisses lingered, and the feel of him against her, but she pushed the thought out of her mind.

Brooke took a white terry-cloth robe from the closet and slipped it over her shoulders. Holding it together in the front, she returned to the living room. Chong had opened his briefcase and spread a towel on the dining room table. His bottles were arranged on the sideboard; his coat hung over the back of the chair. Now he rolled up his sleeves, smiling the same tight smile.

Brooke slipped out of the robe. She lay on her stomach on the towel, arms folded beneath her head, and waited. Soon she felt Chong's strong hands on her back and smelled the fragrant ointment that he used. Expertly, his fingers moved up her spine, massaging the sore muscles and then, when they were engorged with blood, kneading the stiffness and pain out of them. Brooke had been told that her back pains were psychosomatic, that all she needed was a good psychiatrist, but it was Mr. Chong who always brought her relief.

She slipped into the state of semiconsciousness that had become so familiar to her. She thought of Sam again and for a moment imagined that it was he who massaged her, but then her mind focused, as usual, on George Bynum. She could not escape him, even in death.

Brooke closed her eyes. At least a hundred times she had replayed the scene at Crispin's when she and George worked late, as if by going over it again and again she might somehow change it. She wished that it had never happened. They had been unpacking part of the Maddow collection, and Brooke was genuinely thrilled to be close to such priceless, beautiful antiquities. George had taken a Roman perfume jar from a crate; she clearly remembered the look of pleasure on his face, mixed with a kind of daring.

"Here," George had said, offering her the jar.

When Brooke showed reluctance to handle something so valuable—and vulnerable—George had pressed it into her hands.

"Look, you can hold it, you can touch it, you can feel it. You don't have to be afraid of it."

The words had sexual allure. Brooke remembered the smooth, cool, solid feel of the perfume jar, and the excitement it engendered. George was very good at setting the proper scene, although Brooke had not been resistant to him. Speaking softly and authoritatively, he had begun to describe the artisan who had made the jar.

"Now here's this man who lived five hundred years before Christ. He probably didn't even know how to read and write. He never traveled more than a few miles from the village where he was born . . ."

Brooke had felt a great sadness. "We'll never know his name."

"He wasn't even an artist in the way we think of artists today. And he has made something that has outlived Caesar, that outlived Loreno de' Medici, that outlived Napoleon! And if you don't drop it," he had added affectionately, "it will outlive you and me."

The rest of the evening she remembered with utter clarity: George took the jar from her and gently laid it on its side in the packing crate. Then he kissed her. Brooke had been alone for a long time. She allowed him to unbutton her blouse and slip a hand over her breast, fascinated. He seemed so sure of himself; once Brooke had begun to kiss him back, she couldn't stop.

The love-making had been an anti-climax. Afterward, as they lay together, George had touched her in the small of her back, as if he had sensed the point of her greatest vulnerability.

"What's the matter?" he had asked, when Brooke tried to slip from beneath his hand. "Is something wrong with your back?"

"I hurt it a long time ago."

"When you were a kid?"

"When I was eighteen."

"Was it a car accident?"

"No," said Brooke, wanting to change the subject.

George had a built in sensor that focused on other people's weakness. "Was there something upsetting about it?"

"It was nothing."

"Were you in Italy?"

"Florence. It was nothing, really." She leaned across and began to kiss him passionately, silencing him.

Brooke felt an affectionate pat on her buttocks. Roused from her reverie, she looked up into Chong's smiling face. The massage was over. Brooke was as surprised as Chong when she realized that tears were running down her cheeks.

9

Empty cardboard cartons littered the floor of Sam's living room. They had contained shrimp and green peppers, sweet and sour pork, and fluffy rice, all brought from the Hunan restaurant on Columbus Avenue. Sending out for Chinese food was a tradition with Sam and his mother. As long as he could remember, they had settled down together with chopsticks once a week to discuss Sam's school work or his girl problems and, later, his career.

Tonight felt like old times, except that the stakes had changed and an element of danger had been introduced. For two hours they had gone over George Bynum's analyses, reviewing the notations Sam had made on the blackboard. Grace lay back in the chair, smoking another of the chain of cigarettes that followed her meal; she assumed a contemplative pose. He had saved the dream for last, recognizing it as the most fertile territory, hoping that his mother would see there something he had missed.

Sam's concentration faltered again and again. He kept thinking of Brooke, the smell and the feel of her, and the warmth of her kiss. He hoped Grace would not notice this uncharacteristic irrationality: psychiatrists were not supposed to get carried away by beautiful, younger women.

Grace got up and began to pace while Sam read the last of his notes aloud.

". . . the box lands on the floor. Bynum looks around, and the little girl is there, waiting for him. And that's when he wakes up."

Sam thought of Brooke again. Was she the girl in Bynum's dream, or was the connection only in Sam's mind? Did George Bynum have some other secret life that he had managed to hide from his psychiatrist for two years, some relationship so passionate—or psychotic—that it led to his murder? Sam hoped that was the case and that his mother would see some evidence of it.

"All right," said Grace, stamping out her cigarette on her plate. "Since we don't have anything in the way of associations, let's have a go at the traditional stuff. Now the box is a woman."

Without missing a beat, Sam said, "Green, jealousy."

"So we start by considering the possibility that we are dealing with a jealous woman."

"And, since Bynum puts the box into his pocket, I can only assume that he thinks he has some sort of control over the jealous woman."

Grace nodded. So far they were working in harmony.

"Until something goes wrong," Grace said, "and she gets loose. What about the little girl?"

Sam didn't answer.

"Did he tell you why he was frightened of her?"

"No. I got the dream out of him, that's all." He wished now that he had asked the question. But

Sam had his own ideas. "My guess is that the little girl's a surrogate for the mother, or a sister . . ."

"No, no," said Grace, interrupting him. Sam felt a touch of annoyance. He had not been happy with that analysis himself, but his mother could be dogmatic.

"We are probably dealing with a woman who on the surface seems childlike and innocent but underneath is capable of extreme violence."

Grace put another cigarette between her lips and fired up her slim gold lighter. Sam could see her growing excitement: Grace had become Nancy Drew, the amateur sleuth. Sam discounted her analysis of the problem. Bynum had hated and feared either his mother or his sister, and that was that.

"Sam," Grace began, quite serious, "I think you should call the police."

His annoyance gave way to anger. "With what? What kind of evidence do I have?" Sarcastically, he added, "A green box and a little girl who's mean to her teddy bear? C'mon, Grace, you know better than that."

His reaction surprised Sam, as well as his mother. She looked at him closely, and Sam felt the old power of her scrutiny. It was very difficult to hide something from Grace Rice.

"Well," she said casually, "if you're not going to the police, then why are you getting mixed up in all this?"

The implication was that Sam had become emotionally involved. He refused to accept that.

"Bullshit," he said. "I told you before; I spent

almost two years, twice a week, talking to this man.
I want to know why he was killed."

"I don't think so." She calmly puffed on her
cigarette.

"What's that supposed to mean?"

"It's supposed to mean that I don't think you're
doing any of this because of your attachment to
Mr. Bynum. He was obviously a grandiose, narcis-
sistic man, and I'm surprised somebody didn't kill
him before now." She sighed and added, "The
trouble is, when something like this happens, we
feel responsible. So we say to ourselves, 'Okay, if
the patient wouldn't let me help him when he was
alive, now he doesn't have any choice.'"

There was some truth in what she said.

"But Bynum's problem wasn't psychological,"
she went on. "He wasn't worried about losing his
job or something like that—he was scared to
death!"

"Don't be so melodramatic, Mother."

She picked up the folder holding the notes on
George Bynum. "Three days after this," she said,
tapping it, "the patient ends up with his throat cut.
That's melodramatic?"

"The contents of Bynum's dream are purely symbolic, in my opinion. You know as well as I do
that the woman in the bedroom represents his
mother. I told you, the man had a complicated and
unresolved Oedipal problem."

She tried another angle. "Let's say there was
something else going on, something besides the
Oedipal thing. Let's say that the blood and the staircase are sexual references. Now if that's true, it

would indicate that the person he was afraid of was a woman in his present life."

Sam disagreed. "Those references are nothing but screens for someone in the past."

"Absolutely wrong! It's someone in real life, in the here-and-now. Your patient was killed by a woman."

Grace had not talked to the police, and Sam hadn't told her of their findings. Now the accuracy of her analysis stunned him.

But he said, "That's nothing but a cheap, obvious, analytic guess."

"Sam, remember, you didn't kill him. You were only his doctor; there was only so much you could do."

"I suppose you're right." He didn't really want her to get any closer to the truth.

"Sam?"

"Yes, Mother?"

"That is the reason for your involvement in all this, isn't it?"

"Right on the button," he said, sounding miserable even to himself.

"How interested are you in that girl?"

"What girl?" he asked.

Grace regarded him skeptically.

"Oh, *her*? You mean Brooke Reynolds? I don't know what you're getting at."

"Are you in love with her?"

"With Brooke? No, not at all." He wished he had never invited Grace to come over. She sat down again, crossed her legs and folded her hands in her lap. She stared at the litter of food cartons and cigarette butts, thinking.

Finally she said, "When Sarah left you, besides all the feelings of loss and of anger which are natural, there had to be a terrible sense of guilt. A feeling that you, above all people, should have been able to see the warning signals and prevent what happened. Now, Sam, I've got to be honest with you. I don't think you've ever dealt with that."

Sam didn't want to hear it. "Mother. . . ."

"Just listen to me, Sam. You know as well as I do that when you love somebody, and they leave you, very often the only way you can deal with it is by focusing on—even becoming obsessed with—someone else. I think you've lost your sense of objectivity. If you don't look out, you're going to put yourself in a very dangerous situation." And she added urgently, "Go to the police, please."

"What if she didn't do it?" he asked. He felt drained.

"What if she did?"

Sam began to clear the cartons away. He walked into the kitchen and stood for a moment with his hands on the edge of the sink. The rational and emotional sides of his mind were warring, with some heavy losses.

"Well?" Grace called, from the living room.

"I'll think about it."

He heard her getting her coat from the closet. She was upset, he knew; that was unworthy of Sam. He went out into the hall and put his arm around Grace's shoulders. He realized that she was getting frail, and older.

"Mom," he said, leading her back to the sofa, "do you remember the time when I was going to quit school and play pro ball, when I got that offer from a Class A team in Knoxville?" It had been the high point of his life and the realization of his earliest dreams of playing professional baseball. It seemed like yesterday.

"I called," he went on, "and told you what I wanted to do. I think it was the only time you ever walked out on a patient."

Sam had been a student at Yale, serious, dedicated, even popular. But there were unresolved tensions in his own mind. On one hand, he wanted to be a professional like his mother. On the other hand, he wanted something entirely different. He knew how hard Grace worked, the stress and disappointment of trying to get people to heal themselves through reflection and analysis, and he wasn't at all sure that was the way he wanted to spend his life. Playing professional baseball had a powerful appeal.

"You took the first train to New Haven," he told her. "Do you remember that?"

Grace seemed troubled by the memory. "If you had really wanted to quit school—"

"I wouldn't have called," he said, finishing her analysis. "I know. And you sat with me for six hours and let me talk myself out of it."

Grace started to protest, but Sam wouldn't let her. He wasn't criticizing her; he just wanted her to understand how he felt now.

"And you were right! I've never been sorry. I *am* a better shrink than I would have been a second baseman. But if I had played baseball, even if I had never gotten to the majors, I would have known I was a better baseball player than you. But this way, we both know that I'm never going to be as good a shrink as you are."

"Oh, no. *No*." Her protest was automatic, but it still bothered her, Sam could see.

He patted her arm affectionately. "That's not the point I'm making, Mom. What I want to say is, I closed some kind of door that day you came to New Haven. And I've been closing doors ever since. What I'm trying to do"—he paused, trying to sort it out in his own mind—"and maybe it's irrational; maybe it *is* dangerous . . . but I have to do this."

"Oh, Sam," said Grace, and he knew she understood. She reached up and gave him a peck on the cheek. "Be careful."

They looked at one another, mother and son, without the diplomas, credentials, and success; they had been through a lot together.

Suddenly Sam wanted to be alone. "Oh, Christ," he said, glancing at his watch. "I've got an eight-thirty patient tomorrow."

Grace knew he was lying and told one herself.

"Me, too. I have to go."

Sam walked her to the elevator. There were many things she might have said, but Grace Rice knew when it was best to say nothing at all. Sam watched the elevator door close on his mother's knowing, sad smile.

He went back to the apartment and sat for several minutes beside the telephone. The card Detective Vitucci had given him lay beside it on the table. If he dialed the number, he could eliminate any risk to himself and possibly help the police find Bynum's murderer. They would take Brooke in for questioning, and if she was innocent, they would probably let her go. But maybe they would not let her go. Maybe the circumstantial evidence would be too great. Maybe Vitucci would charge her with the crime, since he had no one else to charge.

Sam opened the drawer and took out the Manhattan telephone directory. When life gets boring, he told himself, you have to risk it. He owed it to Brooke, as well as to himself, to talk to her again. In a curious way, he owed it to George Bynum, too. As a psychiatrist, Sam was supposedly able to comfort as well as cure. Brooke had some terrible weight on her mind, something, he suspected, that was only partially connected with Bynum. If she would only open up to him, he might be able to help her. He might also be able to eliminate her as a suspect in the murdering, opening other avenues for the police in the process.

He opened the heavy directory and thumbed through the pages until he found the listings for Reynolds. He ran his thumb down the column, missing Brooke's listing the first time. Then he found it: B. Reynolds, on Eighty-first Street.

Sam dialed the number. He realized that his mouth had gone dry. The phone began ringing; the longer it took Brooke to reach it, the greater his impatience grew. He couldn't tolerate the idea of not speaking to her again that night. Immediately, in fact. What if Brooke was herself in danger, if her secret had something to do with Bynum's death that no one but the murderer suspected?

The phone rang and rang.

10

The old townhouse sat between Fifth Avenue and Madison, an elegant Georgian tribute to some family of wealth in the previous century. It had probably been converted to apartments fifty years before, and not much work had been done on the place since. The house number could not be seen from the street. Sam had to climb the steps and peer beneath the empty lamp socket to make it out. There were no lights at all on the upper floors, and the one in the vestibule burned dully.

He opened a door of heavy glass protected by elaborately twisted wrought iron. The brass handle had been worn smooth; the latch didn't work at all. The black and white tiles in the vestibule were cracked, with pieces missing. There was no doorman. A buzzer system had been installed haphazardly—a row of doorbells screwed into the rich, dark panelling, with brass slots for the names. Half of them were empty.

Sam ran his finger down the list. He found Brooke's name and pressed the button. Then he turned to the inside door, which was locked, hoping that she would come down and let him in.

There was no sign of life in the foyer. Through filthy glass he could see a huge fireplace with a carved mantle and marble benches. The tattered carpet led up a broad staircase to deeper shadow. The carved faces of deities and animals assumed fantastic shapes in the half light. Sam thought he saw movement on the stairs and then realized that flaws in the glass gave that illusion.

He rang again. The buzzer did not sound that would unlock the door and let him in; no one came. Sam stepped back into the night air. Cars passed at the corner of Madison, but Eight-first Street was deserted. George Bynum had been killed on a street just like it, just a few blocks uptown.

He wondered where Brooke could be. She had an appointment, she had said; maybe she had not yet returned home. He didn't want to wait in that dim vestibule, and there were no bars or restaurants in the neighborhood. He decided to walk a bit and come back later. An urgency had entered the aftermath of the Bynum murder. He had to talk to Brooke that night.

Sam walked west to Fifth Avenue and headed uptown, toward the Metropolitan. Huge banners hung from the top of the building, announcing the treasures on exhibit inside. Spotlights flooded the broad front steps of the museum, which was locked and empty at this hour. Sam passed on the other side of Fifth, alone at that famous intersection. He considered walking up as far as the Guggenheim Museum, then cutting across to Park and walking back downtown to Eighty-first Street. Brooke might have returned by then.

On impulse, Sam looked behind him. Across the street and half a block away a woman stopped at the foot of the Metropolitan steps. She had been walking in the same direction as he, and she seemed to be watching him. She wore a tailored black coat and a scarf that covered her hair and draped her face in shadow.

It looked like Brooke Reynolds. Sam turned and started toward her, about to wave, but the woman turned at the same time and walked away down Fifth.

Sam crossed the street, following her. A man walking his Afghan stared suspiciously at him, as if Sam were a mugger or a car thief. He walked a little faster and then called after her: "Brooke!"

If she heard him, she gave no indication. She passed out of the Metropolitan's spotlights and into the shadow of the trees lining Central Park. She even walked like Brooke Reynolds. To Sam's amazement, she turned and started down the steps, into the park, unhurried and apparently without fear. There was a dream-like quality in the woman's presence, as if she were somehow untouchable.

By the time Sam reached the stairs, she had disappeared. He could see nothing but the walkway leading down toward the lake and a pool of light beneath the first lamppost. He was torn between fear and curiosity. If it really was Brooke, what was she doing in that jungle in the middle of the night? She was certainly in danger, and Sam would have to help. The park was unsafe even during the day. During the night it teemed wtih armed gangs and men who would murder for a few dollars. No one entered it then except those who were desperate—or insane.

He descended the steps and moved cautiously down the path toward the lake. Nothing moved in the light beneath the lampposts; the shadows of the trees and bushes breathed an eerie menace. Sam had never done anything so foolhardy. In spite of being afraid, he felt a rush of adrenaline that exhilarated him, forcing him further down the path.

A lone figure stood on the far side of the little lake, the black coat and yellow scarf clearly visible. Sam wanted to call out to her again, but that was dangerous, too. This time he was sure that she saw him; she almost semed to beckon with her head as she turned away and started down another path.

Sam crossed the narrow bridge, staying in the shadows, and turned into the path. He couldn't see her, but he could clearly hear her high heels on the concrete as she moved away steadily but unhurriedly. What had seemed to be strange behavior now struck him as demented. Or was it calculated? Did she need protection, or was she leading him into some situation from which he might not return?

The questions swarmed in his mind as he followed her. Most of all, he wanted to know if the woman was Brooke. In some vague way, Sam felt that if he could solve that question, he could solve the others as well—including the riddle of Bynum's murder.

The path led beneath an overpass. The lamp on the far side of the tunnel cast a pale light, but under the overpass the darkness was almost total. He stopped and listened. The footsteps had ceased. A breeze rattled the branches overhead. He could hear the sound of distant traffic, and nothing else.

"Brooke?"

Silence. Sam walked to the tunnel entrance.

Water dripped somewhere nearby. The light on the far side beckoned. He took a deep breath and entered the darkness. His own footsteps sounded deafening. Halfway through he paused again, certain that he had heard something, afraid to be proven right. He held his breath, but the breathing continued.

Someone stood very near him.

"Brooke?" he whispered, in terror.

A dark shape moved across the light at the end of the tunnel. Sam started to speak again, but at that moment he saw the glint of the light on steel and realized that a knife blade hovered inches from his face. The person grasped the shoulder of his jacket and shoved Sam up against the moist stones in the wall. He looked into the hideous, unshaven face of a young stranger, distorted by hunger and what Sam recognized as the ravages of drug addiction.

"All right, you son of a bitch," the young man said in a hoarse voice full of sickness and pain, "give me all your money."

Terror gave way to fright and a kind of gratitude. At least the man was not a crazed killer. Sam might be able to escape with his life, if he could calm the mugger.

"All right," Sam said, trying to keep the tremor out of his voice. "Okay, I'll tell you what, I've got about fifty or sixty cents in change . . ."

He fished it out of his pocket, feeling the cold steel of the knife blade against his throat. The man knocked the change contemptuously out of Sam's hand, and it scattered over the bricks.

"Oh, yeah," Sam said, digging into the other

pocket, and coming up with a wad of bills. "That's about seventeen, eighteen dollars . . ."

"I'll take that!"

The mugger snatched the money. Then he got a grip on Sam's wrist. Sam wore an inexpensive digital watch, and he willingly handed that over, too. His hands were shaking and his mouth dry, but he had glimpsed a rare advantage in being mugged. Sam had allowed a strange woman, possibly a murderess, to lure him into the park, and now maybe this guy would help him get out alive.

"Now, look," he told the young man, "I know this sounds a little crazy, but I'd like you to do me a favor."

The mugger looked at Sam suspiciously. With a little prompting, he might kill Sam himself.

"My wallet," Sam said, sweetening the deal. "You want my wallet, don't you?"

He took it out and thumbed through the credit cards.

"Here's American Express, Visa, Mastercharge . . ."

The man grabbed the wallet and stuffed it into his Windbreaker pocket without bothering to look for the cash. Sam was obviously the best mark he had had in a long time.

The knife remained against Sam's throat. "Hey, look man," said the owner, "you try something with me, and you're dead. Okay?"

"Oh, no, no, no," Sam insisted. "Just do me a favor. I know this does sound crazy, like I said, but I'd just like you to stay here and watch. Make sure I get out of the park safe, okay?"

But the mugger ignored the request. He had taken

an obvious interest in Sam's jacket—a Pierre Cardin that he had bought the week before at Bloomingdale's.

"I want that coat," he said.

"What?" Sam thought he saw movement in the shadows behind the mugger.

"I said I want the coat."

"Sure." Sam stripped it off. "You got it."

The mugger draped the jacket over his arm. At last the knife was lowered.

"Beat it!"

"What about the favor?"

The man took another step toward him, knife raised. "I ain't gonna tell you again. Now get your ass out of here."

"All right."

Sam was only too happy to obey. He walked quickly back in the direction he had come from. When he reached the light beyond the tunnel, he turned and said, "Thanks a lot."

There was no response from the darkness. Relieved, Sam sprinted back to the street.

The young man closed the knife and slipped it into the pocket of his jeans. Then he slipped into Sam's jacket. It fit him well and gave him a feeling of importance. He would cross the park toward the west and then walk over to Columbus Avenue, where he could score. The heroin dealer would be impressed with the new threads.

He walked toward the far end of the tunnel, away from the man he had robbed. He paused, still in the shadow, and began to go through the wallet, searching for more money. He heard a foot scrape against the sidewalk and looked up in time to see a dark shape loom. He could not believe it, a woman in a scarf in the park at night, walking right up to him.

He took his time reaching for his shiv. This would be the easiest score he had ever made. But before he could get the weapon out, he realized that something was terribly wrong. The woman's hand swept forward, and too late he saw the long, ugly blade of a butcher knife.

11

For the second time in a week, Detective Joseph Vitucci had to get up at dawn and drive into Manhattan from Queens in his unmarked cruiser. The telephone call had come from Central Intelligence Division, and it was remarkably like the first one regarding the victim, the location, and the nature of the crime. The similarities nagged at him as he crossed the Fifty-ninth Street Bridge and took Park Avenue north.

He entered Central Park by the service road. The crime scene was not difficult to find. Three NYPD cruisers were parked bumper to bumber on the path, and the white van from the coroner's office sat with two wheels on the grass, the double back doors thrown open, the red light revolving. Vitucci hoped that Murray was off duty today. Murray could be a real pain in the ass so early in the morning.

Vitucci parked in line and stepped out into the crisp autumn air. It was going to be another beautiful day. The lake actually looked clean, reflecting the blue sky. Birds that had not left for the southward flight perched in the dogwood trees. Joggers in brightly colored sweat suits, some with earphones attached to tape players strapped to their waists, ran along the higher path, unaware that a body lay in the tunnel below them. They formed a moving tableau against a backdrop of trees and distant skyscrapers. Other joggers clustered around the mouth of the tunnel, aware that something grim and horrible lay inside, their faces reflecting confusion and some fear.

Vitucci was relieved to see two uniformed policeman turn the onlookers away. Inside the tunnel, half a dozen flashlights moved over the ground, searching for clues. A body lay sprawled on the damp bricks. He approached the group, and two men from Forensic made way for him. There was nothing for them to say: the cause of death was brutally obvious. Vitucci looked from the wounds to the victim's face—a bum, although he wore a nice jacket. Vitucci felt a faint glimmering of hope. The last person killed like this had been well-to-do and well-connected. Maybe there was no link between the two.

The victim's personal effects had been collected and placed in glassine bags. The bags had been placed in the evidence box, which sat at the feet of the driver from the coroner's office. Vitucci looked up into Murray's grinning face, and his heart sank.

Without a word, he picked up the evidence box and carried it out into the sunlight. He sat down on the steps and began to open the bags. The first contained a knife, an ugly-looking switchblade with a broken handle. The second bag contained a wallet. Vitucci extracted a credit card from it, read the name on the card and said, "Shit!"

Murray just beamed.

*　　*　　*

When Sam came out on the street, on his way to the office, he saw a police car parked in front of the apartment building and a burly uniformed cop talking to the doorman. The cop turned and said, "Doctor Rice, just a minute. Detective Vitucci from Homicide Central wants to talk to you."

"I'm on my way to work."

"It won't take but a few minutes, sir."

He already had the door of the cruiser open. Another cop was riding shotgun, staring straight ahead, cradling a Styrofoam cup of coffee in his lap. Sam hesitated and then stepped into the car. It smelled of cigarette smoke.

"What's this all about?" Sam asked.

"There's been a murder."

The cop made a U-turn and accelerated, heading toward the park. He casually reached up and turned on the siren; the shriek almost caused a cyclist to fall off his machine.

Sam felt a cold, hollow place in the pit of his stomach. "Who was murdered?" he managed.

"A bum, looks like. Vitucci will tell you about it."

Cars pulled over to make way for the cruiser. Sam's mind raced even faster. He had spent a sleepless night, worrying about the woman in the park and the mugger. Sam could have been killed as well as robbed and humiliated. He had taken a terrible chance and was no wiser than before.

Now it sounded like the mugger had killed someone else. The police probably found Sam's wallet near the scene of the crime; he had some explaining to do.

When they arrived at the overpass, Sam was surprised to find the section of walkway there so open and unthreatening. Except for all the police cars and commotion, it was obviously a peaceful spot. Vitucci sat on the steps with a man in a white technician's coat, examining objects in little plastic bags.

" 'Morning, Doctor," Vitucci said. "I've got something of yours here." He picked up Sam's wallet. "You should be more careful with these credit cards. American Express—"

"I told him," said the man in the white coat, as if he and Sam were old friends. "He wouldn't listen."

Sam had no idea what he was talking about.

"Right, Murray," said Vitucci, otherwise ignoring him. "Mastercharge—"

"That's a five you owe me."

"Not now, Murray. Visa, Diner's Club—"

"Twelve wounds," Murray went on. "Whew! The first had to be the throat. After that the victim goes into shock, and then—"

"*Murray.* Let's not talk about it now."

Murray shrugged, his feelings hurt. "Sure, sure . . ." Vitucci handed Sam the wallet. His head throbbed as he examined it. The man had said something about twelve wounds.

"Anything missing?"

Sam shook his head.

"Now to the cash. This guy had two hundred and seventy-four dollars and ninety-three cents on him. Any of that belong to you?"

Finally Sam saw the light: the man who had mugged him had himself been murdered.

"I don't know exactly how much I had on me last night. It couldn't have been more than about seventeen dollars and change." The rest of the cash was still in the wallet.

Vitucci handed him a list of possessions that had been found on the body and belonged to Sam. They had missed the watch and the jacket, but he didn't care.

"Your personal effects will be returned to you as soon as Forensic is through with them. A cashier's check will be sent to you for the money. As for the coat . . . tough luck."

So Vitucci knew it was Sam's.

"Will you sign, please?"

Sam did as he was asked. The jacket, in a separate container, was covered with blood. He watched as two more technicians hoisted a black body bag into the waiting van and slammed the back doors.

"Doctor?" said Murray, unable to contain himself any longer. "Do you want to know what I think?"

Sam didn't, but he knew he had no choice. Murray obviously considered himself a professional medical man.

"I think we're dealing with a multiple personality." Murray turned to Vitucci, and explained, "That's where the behavior of an individual is split up, and—"

"*Murray!*"

"Sorry. Just trying to help."

"So," Vitucci said, "would you mind telling me why you were out here last night?"

"I went for a walk."

"You went for a walk?"

That was too flimsy an excuse even for Vitucci.

"I've been having some problems with a patient," Sam repeated. "I went for a walk to try to work some things out."

"In Central Park? At eleven thirty at night?"

"Well, actually—" Sam paused, thinking. He owed the police an explanation—"I know this sounds nuts, but I thought I saw somebody."

"What do you mean, you thought you saw somebody?"

"Well, I was having trouble with a patient. I guess I went farther in the park than I realized."

"That's it?" said Vitucci.

"You're kidding," added Murray. They both stared at him in disbelief. Fortunately, Vitucci's beeper went off at that moment.

"Murray, do me a favor," said Vitucci, still watching Sam. "Call the squad and see what they want."

"You got it."

As soon as Murray was gone, the detective asked, "Who's the woman?"

"A former patient," Sam lied.

Vitucci slowly shook his head. He smiled unpleasantly and stepped close to Sam.

"Doctor, I think there's something you don't understand. Someone tried to kill you last night."

"I don't buy that," Sam said, and he didn't buy it. "Look, a patient of mine is murdered, for whatever reasons. A few days later I go for a walk, and by coincidence I end up in the park and get mugged."

"I don't think so. I don't think—I *know*. George

Bynum was screwing around. Things got out of hand. He had a fight, and this girl kills him."

"Even if you were right, why would she want to kill me?"

"Because George Bynum was a patient of yours," Vitucci said. "And because she can never be sure that he didn't say something to you about her. Otherwise, she's in the clear. She and Bynum were very careful that people at Crispin's didn't know about them."

Murray had returned, but Vitucci put out his hand, silencing him. "Wait a minute."

Sam said, "The guy who mugged me got mugged himself. He put up a struggle and got killed. That kind of thing happens every day."

"Then why wasn't anything stolen from him?"

"I don't know." Sam didn't want to deal with that. "Maybe whoever did it got scared off before he could go through the pockets."

"Then how come the weapon used and the pattern of wounds are virtually the same as they were with George Bynum?"

Sam couldn't answer that. He had to talk to Brooke Reynolds before the police did.

"First," Vitucci said, grasping his forefinger, "this guy was murdered because he was wearing your coat. Second, I just lost five bucks to this schnook"—and he hooked a thumb at Murray—"because of the similar wounds. I'm telling you, Doctor, it's the same woman."

"And I got another twenty bucks," said Murray cheerfully, "that says she's not finished yet."

12

Several times during the long day, Sam found himself staring at the telephone, wishing to hear the sound of Brooke's voice. But he wanted to be able to see her face when he told her about the mysterious woman and the murder in Central Park. If Brooke was innocent, he would know it. As a psychiatrist, he had a refined sense of a person's truthfulness, or so he had always thought.

But doubt nagged at him; it threatened to disrupt his sessions with his patients. Sam had not been very good, for instance, in seeing through George Bynum. Bynum had never been serious about his analysis and had treated the sessions from the beginning like a contest. He had not intended to flatter Sam by saying that Brooke would have liked the doctor; instead, he hoped to demean him. Bynum did his best to manipulate Sam and exploit the situation for his own advantage. He even used his appointments with Sam as a cover for his affair with Brooke.

Bynum had not been a man to accept losing well. Brooke tried to break off the relationship, she said, but Bynum *kept pushing*. What exactly had she meant by that? How had Bynum pushed? Sam realized that he himself knew almost nothing about

Brooke, that he had instinctively given her the benefit of the doubt. It was a wonder that someone hadn't murdered Bynum long before, Grace had said. But now there were two murders to deal with.

Sam worked late and then took a cab to Eighty-first Street. The townhouse looked as shabby as it had the night before, but a light burned in the top row of windows.

He climbed the steps and entered the vestibule. A copy of the *New York Times* lay unclaimed on the tiles; the murder of a bum in Central Park would never make it into the ordered gray columns of the *Times.* Sam pushed the button next to Brooke's name and waited anxiously. When there was no answer, he rang the bell again.

Finally he heard a rush of static and Brooke's voice: "Who is it?"

"It's me, Sam. I have to talk to you."

After a long pause, she said, "Well . . . okay," and buzzed him through.

It wasn't the response he had hoped for. He stepped into the dim foyer and started up the stairs, on carpet worn through in the center. He looked down at the elaborately carved mantle and the marble benches; the house had a timeless quality. It seemed irrelevant to the world beyond the heavy glass door—a case of arrested development.

Sam climbed to the top floor. One of the doors on the landing stood ajar.

"Brooke?" he said tentatively.

There was no answer. The number on the door was the right one, and Sam walked into the apartment. He saw walls painted a dark ultramarine blue and a Japanese print of a Buddhist monk staring

104

down at him. Three beautiful Roman heads stood on the mantle.

In front of the fireplace, stretched out on a table and covered by only a towel, was Brooke. Her long blonde hair hung down almost to the floor. Her chin was propped on her hands, and she smiled at Sam.

"Hi."

Sam just stood there, speechless. He was overcome by Brooke's beauty—and by the fact that an Oriental man stood next to her, fully clothed, staring at Sam.

"Mr. Chong," said Brooke, "this is Dr. Rice. Dr. Rice, Mr. Chong."

She made the introduction seem perfectly natural. Mr. Chong smiled for the first time and bowed slightly at the waist. Sam found himself doing the same thing. Then Mr. Chong bent over Brooke, put his hands on the small of her back, and began to massage.

"Where were you last night?" Brooke asked. "I went back to Crispin's and tried to get some work done. I tried to call you."

Sam had meant to ask the same question. But Brooke had already explained her whereabouts the night before.

"I went for a walk," he said.

"Oh, really?" She seemed to be playing with him. "You were gone forever. I called several times."

"It was a long walk." That was true.

All his doubts about her faded as he watched Mr. Chong perform his task. Brooke smiled at his discomfort. She seemed slightly embarrassed herself, yet pleased that Sam was there.

"It wasn't anything important," she said.

They both said, at the same moment, "I was just wondering—" and broke off in laughter. For a long time they looked at one another.

"I was just wondering," she said finally, "if you were all right."

"I'm fine. How about you?"

She nodded. Still smiling, she turned and rested her cheek on her hands.

To cover his embarrassment, Sam asked, "Do you do this sort of thing regularly?"

"I have a problem with my back. Mr. Chong comes over most nights."

Sam wanted to say more, but Mr. Chong's presence prevented him. He felt a strong attraction to Brooke and was certain that she felt it, too.

He turned toward the door.

"When will I see you?" she asked.

Sam just shrugged.

"There's a very important auction at Crispin's tomorrow night, of some things in the Maddow estate. I'll be bidding for an Italian client. One or two of the pieces should go for more than a million dollars. If you've never been to an auction, you might find it exciting."

"I'm sure I would," Sam said.

"It begins at eight o'clock."

He nodded, starting to leave.

"Sam?"

"Yeah?"

"What did you want to see me about?"

"Nothing."

He could leave it like that, he thought. Or he could take a chance and follow his own emotions.

106

"Would you like to have dinner?" he asked. "When you're finished."

"Yes, I would." Brooke seemed relieved and happy.

"I'll wait downstairs. It was nice meeting you, Mr. Chong."

Chong nodded while he worked. Sam went out and walked down to the foyer. He sat on one of the marble benches, which was hard and cold, and looked at the dusty figures carved in the mantlepiece. The fireplace had not held logs for many years.

After a few minutes, Chong came down the stairs wearing an overcoat and carrying a heavy briefcase. He nodded again and went out into the night. Sam expected Brooke to follow. He waited for what seemed like a long time. There was no sound in the old house, no coming and going of other tenants, just the distant blare of car horns and, somewhere, the murmur of recorded music.

Sam heard footsteps on the stairs. He looked up and saw Brooke on the landing. She wore a skirt and blouse, and carried her coat over one arm. She had put her hair in a French roll, accentuating the delicate features of her face. Brooke's skin was very white, her lips a dark red.

Sam said, "Jesus!"

"Don't I look all right?"

"You look wonderful."

She walked down to him. Sam took her arm, and together they walked out to the street. He had made no plans—the dinner invitation had been as much a surprise to him as it had to Brooke. She looked so stunning that Sam wanted to take her to

Lutèce, but they would never get into the restaurant without reservations. Instead, he hailed a taxi, and they rode across town to an excellent French restaurant on the West Side.

They talked very little in the cab. Sam held Brooke's hand, feeling like a kid on a first date. In the restaurant, they sat in a corner, their own private space shared only by a fluttering candle flame and, occasionally, the waiter. Sam was impressed with Brooke's knowledge of French, and French food; she was sophisticated without being brash, as only a person could be who had spent a lot of time in Europe. She spoke freely of the years she spent there, mostly in Italy.

Sam was fascinated. Brooke said her mother had been very rich, explaining the fact that Brooke had real art treasures in her apartment, and enjoyed a style of life that would not be possible on her Crispin's salary. Her father had no money at all, she said. He was a painter—probably not a very good one, judging from the way she described his work—and was very charming. "One of those people," Brooke said, without condemnation, "who learns to live among the rich with a great deal of ease." Brooke had adored her father and fought with her mother. Both parents, she said, were dead.

After her father's death, she had moved to London to attend the Corthauld Institute, which had the best art history department in the world. After graduation, she had gone to work for Sothebys, doing much the same thing she would do later at Crispin's. Although Brooke never said so, Sam had the impression that she led an almost reclusive life. An element of mystery surrounded her that the explanations of her past did nothing to dispell. It added to Brooke's already considerable charm. Sam was attracted by the mystery, just as George Bynum must have been.

Sam wanted to ask why she had never married and what she had seen in a philanderer like Bynum. He also wanted to tell her about the second murder and to warn her about Vitucci. But the subject did not go with the romantic setting; Sam didn't want to spoil it.

"What about you?" she asked. "How did you get to be a psychiatrist?"

Both his parents had been psychiatrists, he told her. His father had died while Sam was very young, and Grace had raised him alone. Sam was a Yaley, but he had not been a distinguished student. Then, to his surprise, he began to explain his love of baseball and how he had almost turned pro. Even Sarah didn't know about that.

"I'm still a Yankees fan," he admitted.

"I don't know much about baseball, but I can see you were passionate about it. I like that." She paused and asked, "Why did your wife leave you?"

"It's that obvious, huh, that I didn't leave her?"

"Well, she took half the furniture."

Sam nodded. He didn't like to admit it, but he had been left with an overwhelming sense of failure after Sarah left, as well as the guilt his mother had spoken of.

"She found a cinematographer more interesting than me," he said.

"That's hard to believe."

"Not really. Sarah was an actress. But after we were married, she got tired of acting. Mostly she got tired of other actors, I think, but she was successful enough to have a part in a long-running soap opera. I think she always thought of me as a stable, more intellectual alternative to that life. She wanted to settle down, she said, but after she tried it she didn't like it. In her defense," he added, "I was spending an awful lot of time with my practice."

Brooke smiled at him. "I don't see anything wrong with working hard."

They tarried over the last of the Bordeaux. Sam couldn't put it off any longer.

"There was another murder last night," he said. "In Central Park."

"What do you mean, *another* murder?"

"The man—a bum and a mugger—was killed in the same way George Bynum was. The police think the same person is responsible for both."

Brooke shuddered. She watched Sam closely.

He said, "Vitucci is convinced that the woman who killed them works at Crispin's."

"What do you think?" she asked quietly.

"I think it's very plausible."

"Has my name come up?"

"No," Sam said, "but I wouldn't be surprised if it did. Vitucci will have to question everyone very closely now. If there's anyone else at Crispin's who knew about the two of you, it's bound to surface."

Brooke seemed to arrive at some conclusion on her own, but she wasn't sharing it with Sam.

"How did you know about the murder in the park?" she asked.

Sam could have said that Vitucci told him, which in a way was true. Instead, he said, "I went into

110

the park last night. The victim mugged me before he was killed."

Brooke obviously didn't know whether or not to believe him. Sam quickly told her about the strange woman, the encounter in the tunnel, and his escape. If she was pretending to be amazed, he thought, she was a very good actress.

"But why," she asked, "would you follow a strange woman into the park?"

"She resembled someone I know. I got the impression she wanted me to follow her."

"Who did she resemble?"

"You, Brooke."

Sam could see the realization dawn on her, like a light bulb coming on: Sam was still suspicious of her.

"Did you tell the police?" she asked, a frostiness in her voice. "About mistaking the woman for me?"

"Of course not."

"Why are you protecting me?"

"I don't know." The admission sounded stupid. "I guess I didn't want to see anything happen to you."

"But you still think I killed George Bynum."

"No; I told you that before." The fact was, Sam didn't know what to think.

"But you're not sure," Brooke said.

It was a simple statement of fact. At that moment the waiter arrived with the check, providing Sam with an excuse for not responding. He paid with the American Express card that Vitucci had returned to him and followed Brooke out to the street. He immediately began hailing cabs.

"Sam," Brooke said.

"Taxi!"

"Sam, if you're not sure about me, why are you doing all this?"

"You ask an awful lot of questions."

They stood inches apart without touching. Sam remembered the night before; he was dying to kiss her again.

A cab pulled over, and they climbed in.

"Do you want to go home?" Sam asked.

"I'll go wherever you want to go."

He hesitated and gave the driver his own address. This time he and Brooke did not hold hands.

"Tell me something, Sam," she said, still cold as ice. "What makes you think I won't kill you?"

She was taunting him. Sam, afraid the cabbie would hear her and misunderstand, whispered, "Will you shut up?"

Brooks settled back against the seat, silent and withdrawn. Sam was accustomed to women who became more emotionally involved than he—and who pursued him. But Brooke seemed wary of involvement, and self-sufficient. Sam had become the aggressor, which surprised and excited him. It also made him extremely uneasy—he wanted Brooke, and he was also a little afraid of her.

The cab stopped outside Sam's apartment building. He fished the money out of his pocket, paid the cabbie, and escorted Brooke across the pavement. He let them in with his key, since there was no sign of the doorman.

Inside, Sam called out, "Angelo?"

He must have been in the basement. Brooke said, with a trace of sarcasm, "Nervous?"

Sam didn't answer. He jabbed at the button,

summoning the elevator, and they rode up side by side, staring at the numbers that lit up one by one. They stepped out on Sam's floor, and he fumbled for the key in his jacket pocket. Then he let Brooke precede him into the apartment.

Sam quickly turned on the lamp in the hall. Brooke reached up and fastened the latch on the door, and Sam's heart began to pound.

"You're very self-destructive," she said, still taunting. "Do you know that?"

"Maybe." His tongue felt thick and heavy. "Do you want a drink?"

Brooke shook her head. She came and stood very close to him. Her eyes semed translucent, a beautiful, depthless blue. Sam did not really know who lived behind those eyes.

"You have to be very careful, Sam. You can never tell what I might do."

"You enjoy making fun of me, don't you?"

"No." She was no longer teasing him. "I was so happy with you."

"What do you mean by *was*?"

She looked past him, toward the dark bedroom. "Why couldn't you believe in me? Just a little bit?"

"Brooke," he said quietly, "if you're me, nothing's really simple." Searching for hidden meaning was part of his profession and his personality.

She touched his arm. "But you're scared."

"Maybe."

"Oh, you're very scared. "Look, your hand's shaking."

Sam didn't bother to deny it. She knew a lot more about Sam than he knew about her.

"Why don't you call the police?" she suggested. This time she sounded serious.

They were touching now, their mouths inches apart.

"Poor Sam. You've fallen in love with someone you think is a murderess. I feel sorry for you."

Sam couldn't stand it any longer. He pulled her to him and kissed her full on the mouth. Brooke felt lifeless. He kissed her again. She seemed to awaken slowly, kissing him tentatively in return, then with greater warmth. He moved his lips from hers and down along the nape of her neck. She smelled delicious and somehow forbidding, her breathing growing heavier.

Their lips met again. She kissed him intimately, her tongue seeking his, her hands moving up to the back of his neck and pulling him down to her. Their coats felt like armor, separating their bodies. Sam unbuttoned Brooke's coat and moved his hands up over her blouse.

They stepped apart, panting, watching one another. Brooke slipped out of the coat, letting it fall to the floor. Without a word she walked past him into the bedroom.

Sam hesitated. Then he stripped off his camel's hair overcoat and dropped it.

The bedroom was dark. He could see Brooke's silhouette against the window. She stood very straight, facing him, and he felt fear overcoming his desire. He realized she was unbuttoning the blouse. He began to undress: jacket, tie, shoes. It became a kind of race and Brooke won. He could see only the outline of her body, the fullness of her breasts and her narrow waist as she stood waiting, hands at her sides.

Only the bed separated them. Sam grabbed a handful of coverlet and blanket and peeled them back. He knelt on the mattress; she did the same. Still they didn't touch. His eyes had grown accustomed to the dark, and he could make out a slight smile on Brooke's lips.

They came together violently. Kissing her, Sam moved his hand down over her hips and into the warmth between her legs. He bent over and took one breast and then the other into his mouth. Brooke moaned, taking his erection in her hand and pulling Sam down on top of her. She guided him easily. He expected a frantic encounter, but instead they made love in long, languorous strokes, each one leading him further into oblivion. He was aware only of the incredible warmth of her, and the distant sound of her voice.

Brooke whispered his name over and over again.

13

She woke up at first light. The bedroom was strange, and for a moment she lay without moving, trying to get her bearings. Next to her, Sam slept soundly, his face turned away and one hand trailing on the carpet.

Brooke knew what she had to do. The idea had come to her during the night, and without hesitating she slipped out of bed and put on the clothes she had worn the evening before. She bent over Sam and touched his cheek without waking him. He seemed vulnerable and childlike.

She walked into the kitchen. Like the rest of the apartment, it was ordered and spare, the exact opposite of Brooke's place. The cookbooks were all neatly arranged; the knives were attached to the magnetic holder according to size. She opened the refrigerator. It contained very little food—a loaf of bread, a can of partially used tuna fish, and some oranges. Brooke wasn't hungry, anyway. She was just curious about the way Sam lived.

She found her coat in a pile on the hall floor. She slipped it on, smoothed her hair before the mirror, and left the apartment. A copy of *The New York Times* lay outside the elevator; she wondered if it contained a story about the murder in Central Park.

Downstairs, the doorman smiled at her as she left the building, noticing that she still wore her evening dress. Brooke walked half a block before flagging down a cab, which was no problem at that hour. They sped across the park, through traffic that was already thickening.

Brooke did not direct the driver to her building on Eighty-first Street. Instead, he took her further uptown on the East Side, to a slightly shabby street in the Nineties. She paid him and entered a large apartment building. She had been there once before, and she searched among the name tags until she found the one she wanted: Gail Phillips.

Brooke pushed the buzzer. After a long wait, she heard Gail say sleepily, "Yes?"

"Gail, it's Brooke. Can I come up and talk to you?"

"Sure." Gail was always relaxed.

Brooke pushed through the foyer and boarded the elevator. Of all the people who worked at Crispin's, Gail was the only one with whom Brooke was friendly. Gail had worked there for several years and knew the politics and the personalities of Crispin's much better than Brooke did.

Gail opened her apartment door wearing a robe that was loosely belted, her hair a mess.

"Come in," she said.

As Brooke entered, she saw Gail take a long look at her.

"My," Gail said wryly, "didn't we have a good time last night." Brooke obviously had not slept well.

Brooke decided to ignore that. "I'm sorry to bother you, Gail, but there's no one else to talk to."

"What's the matter?"

Gail didn't sound particularly interested. She crossed to the closet and sorted through her dresses, trying to decide what to wear. The efficiency apartment was tiny, without any framed prints or mementos.

Brooke said, "The police are convinced that a woman working at Crispin's killed George Bynum."

"What?" Gail rubbed her eyes; it was too early in the morning for such serious talk. "Why would somebody there want to kill George? I mean, aside from the fact that he was generally obnoxious?"

"He was having an affair with someone."

"So what else is new?"

"He was having an affair with *me*, Gail."

"With you?"

"We tried to be very careful," Brooke said. "Nobody knew. I was trying to break things off when he was murdered."

"You—and George." Gail just smiled. ". . . *be still, my heart*," she sang.

"Do you think he could have been having an affair with someone else, too."

Gail laughed out loud. She took a skirt from a hanger and crossed to the chest of drawers. She began to search for stockings and a bra.

"There are two hundred women working at Crispin's," Gail said. "George probably hit on at least half of them."

Brooke couldn't believe that she had been such a fool. She needed another suspect to offer to Vitucci, if the detective came looking for her. But one hundred suspects was ridiculous.

"The person who did it was probably very much in love with George," Brooke said, thinking out loud. "Don't you have any idea who it might have been?"

Gail stood before the mirror and brushed her hair while she thought. It was as long and almost as fair as Brooke's hair. They could have been sisters, except that Gail was bigger and stronger and had an easy, intimate way with people that Brooke could never emulate. Brooke envied her that.

"I don't think you should worry about it. You didn't kill George."

"Maybe the person who did knew about George and me," said Brooke. "Maybe she felt betrayed."

Gail began to apply her make-up. She drew faint, precise lines wtih the eyebrow pencil, leaning into the mirror, her hip cocked. They might have been discussing their boyfriends, Brooke thought, instead of murder.

Brooke said, "Sam Rice says the police think the murderess has a split personality."

"Oh, it's *Sam,* is it?"

Gail raised an eyebrow at her in the mirror. Brooke knew she was blushing. Now they were talking about boyfriends.

"Gail, this is serious."

"I'm sorry; I know it's serious. I'll tell you what I'll do—I'll make some discreet inquiries and try to find out which skirts George was chasing at the end. Would that help any?"

"It might," Brooke said.

"And now, young lady, you'd better go home

and change out of your party clothes. We've got a big day ahead of us at Crispin's."

Brooke paused by the door on her way out. "Be careful," she said.

Gail laughed at the suggestion of danger. "You worry too much."

Vitucci knew that luck was important in solving most homicide cases. So far, not one piece of good luck had surfaced in the Bynum case. The psychiatrist had refused to cooperate, and there wasn't much Vitucci could do about that. The world of Crispin's had proved impenetrable to someone of Vitucci's experience; he didn't know what those people were talking about half the time. No one had come forward as an informant; no single name had surfaced that was passionately linked with Bynum at the time of the murder. Yet Vitucci knew instinctively that the civilized exterior harbored a psychopath. He had checked the addresses of every woman between the ages of twenty and forty who worked at Crispin's and was dismayed to learn that a dozen of them lived within a few blocks of the murder scene.

The ones he had interviewed so far all had alibis. Getting information out of them was like pulling teeth. They treated Vitucci like some kind of servant, and he didn't like that. He was a hardworking detective, and he deserved a break.

The break came in the morning after the discovery of the body in Central Park, in the form of a telephone call from a plainclothesman on East Ninety-eighth Street. Vitucci had put out an eighteen-block canvas of policemen to question restaurant and bar owners in the neighborhood, since traces of alcohol had been discovered during the autopsy. But the canvas had turned up a big zero.

"Hey, Joe," said the plainclothesman, "I think I got something for you. The owner of a joint over here says the photograph of the victim looks familiar. He thinks Bynum was in here that night. With a broad."

Vitucci whistled loudly as he drove across town from headquarters.

The bar occupied the basement of an office building long past its prime. A neon Rheingold sign burned in the single window. Inside, little tables with red-and-white checked cloths sat empty in the gloom. A Puerto Rican in a long white apron was sweeping the floor, and a squat, barrel-chested man in his late fifties stood behind the bar, going over receipts from the night before.

The plainclothesman sat drinking coffee and reading the newspaper. He just pointed at the bartender without getting off the stool.

"I'm Detective Vitucci from Homicide." He showed the man his shield. "I understand George Bynum was in here the night he was murdered."

"Not sure it was *the* night, like I told him," he said, jerking his head in the direction of the plainclothesman. "But it was close to it."

"I understand he was with a woman."

The man nodded. He didn't seem eager to help.

"What did she look like?" Vitucci asked.

"A class act. Middle twenties. A blonde."

"Did you get a good look at her face?"

"I guess I did. They had a couple of rounds and

got into quite a little tiff. Didn't seem to care what the other customers thought, either."

"Where did they sit?"

He pointed to the table in the corner. The bar was perfect—anonymous and a little seedy. There was no chance Bynum or his girl would run into anybody there that they knew. A good place for a lovers' spat, one that Vitucci knew had led to murder.

"Would you recognize this young woman," Vitucci asked, "if you saw her again?"

"I guess I would."

Vitucci wasn't interested in guesswork. The bartender knew he was being roped into an investigation, and he didn't like the idea.

"You ought to know," Vitucci told him, "that we suspect this woman of murdering two people. If you can identify her, that means you're in danger, too."

The man swallowed hard and said nothing.

"No, there's nothing to be afraid of," Vitucci went on. "All you have to do is make the ID. You should get somebody else in here tonight to work the bar for you."

"And why would I want to do that?" the man asked.

"Because you're going to an auction," said Vitucci.

14

Crispin's reminded Sam of a theater on opening night. Spotlights lit up the pavement outside, where couples in evening dress stepped out of cabs and long, chauffeur-driven cars. The doormen shuffled and bowed on the curb, welcoming the regular customers as if they were royalty. Some of them undoubtedly were, he thought. Sam had not bothered to put on a tuxedo, wearing instead his usual tweed sport coat, gray flannels and button-down shirt. He was a creature of habit, even if his life had become totally unpredictable.

The sign in the vast foyer directed him to the reception area on the third floor. Sam boarded an elevator that smelled of expensive perfume and was packed with mink coats. There was no chatter among these people—they would soon be challenged to put up money to back their tastes and knowledge in art. The value of Maddow estate had been widely publicized.

Sam rested his head against the richly paneled wall. He wasn't interested in art, but in Brooke, and he couldn't be sure she shared that interest. Her behavior continued to mystify him. He had awakened that morning to find her gone, the passion of the night before like a dream. Brooke hadn't even left a note.

The third floor was already crowded. People stood in tight little groups, poring over Crispin's elaborate catalogue of offerings. There was no sign of Brooke. Gail Phillips sat at the reception desk, talking on one of the ornate telephones; she smiled and waved at Sam. Next to her stood Miss Wilson, the secretary who had been so annoyed by Vitucci's questions. She wore a long gown with a floral pattern. Like most of the women at Crispin's, she was very attractive.

"Doctor Rice?" she said.

"Yes?"

"Brooke asked me to watch out for you. Would you come with me, please?"

Miss Wilson glided through the crowd, toward the door at the far end of the room. Sam could see that the auditorium was already filling up. A heavy easel stood on the low stage, for displaying paintings and prints. A rich mahogany lectern stood off to one side, lit by a bulb in a gold sconce. A bank of telephones on the table would be used for receiving bids from prospective buyers around the world.

She led him across the stairwell and into the cavernous storage room that Sam had seen first with Gail Phillips. Then it had been a busy hub of unpacking and cataloguing, but now most of the lights had been turned off. The scattered crates and furniture cast long shadows over the floor. The room was deserted, except for the two of them.

"You know," Miss Wilson said, "George . . . I mean, Mr. Bynum . . . was really a very wonderful man."

She seemed nervous and anxious to fill the silence. Sam wondered if she, too, had had an affair with his former patient.

"I don't understand," she went on, "why people are saying such horrible things about him. He was really very nice."

They had reached the door on the far side of the room. Miss Wilson paused, and Sam found himself watching her closely. The murders had made him suspicious of everyone. This young woman seemed as unlikely a candidate for murderess as . . . Brooke Reynolds.

She opened the door and held it for Sam. The long hallway led to the porcelain department. The glass cubicles along the way were all dark, the desks piled with papers and a few art objects and choice pieces of china and crystal. A single light burned at the other end of the hall.

"Brooke's in her office, down there. I have to take some catalogues back to reception."

She left him alone. Sam started down the corridor. He had to step around a towering crate, and as he passed it he glimpsed a man inside, one arm raised in a threatening manner. Sam reeled backwards and caught himself against a door. He felt foolish when he realized that the man was made of wax—nothing but a sculpture of a laborer in coveralls.

Sam's nerves were in a worse state than he thought. He took a deep breath and continued on. The hallway grew darker. The band of light from Brooke's office lay across the floor. Sam stopped before he reached the office. He could see Brooke standing at her desk, staring down at some scattered papers. She looked stunning in a dark blue evening gown but there was something disturbing about her concentration. She was so absorbed in what she was doing that she had not even heard him approach.

Sam knocked lightly on the door. Brooke looked up, and he saw that she was terrified. She raked the papers she had been reading toward the open drawer.

"Oh, hi," she said, trying to smile. "Hi!"

He didn't know how to respond. He had caught Brooke in some secret activity, and he was sorry.

"How did you get up here?" she asked, easing the drawer closed with her hip." Before he could answer, she remembered and added, "Heather! Of course; I forgot. I just came up here to get some last minute bids."

She smiled desperately as she locked the desk drawer. She gathered up some manila folders at the other end of the desk, and dropped the key ring on top of them. Then she came around the desk and walked toward him.

Sam started to ask Brooke what she was hiding. But Miss Wilson called to them from the dark hallway.

"Brooke? The auction is starting. We should hurry."

Brooke slipped past Sam and walked quickly away. He took a final look at her office and then shut the door and followed her. Brooke was a different person from the woman he had known the night before. Maybe, Sam reasoned, she was distracted by the importance of the auction and her role in it. After all, Sam had never seen her work. Handling bids by telephone for a customer in another country probably gave her stage fright.

Miss Wilson's presence prevented them from talking. The three of them returned to the reception area. The auditorium was filled, and people drifted up and down the aisles. Brooke led Sam to a seat with a Reserved sign on it. He felt flattered, but before he could thank her, the sharp crack of the auctioneer's gavel silenced the room.

Brooke smiled at Sam and hurried toward the table.

On the carpet at Sam's feet lay her key ring.

"Good evening, ladies and gentlemen," said the auctioneer, an urbane middle-aged man with salt-and-pepper hair swept back and an accent that was vaguely British. His job was probably what George Bynum had aspired to, but Bynum had lacked the air of authenticity required.

"Welcome to Crispin's. This evening we present a sale of important Impressionist and Post-Impressionist paintings, as well as drawings and sculpture, from the Maddow estate. You are reminded that everything is sold as is, and all purchases are subject to a buyer's premium of ten percent. The appropriate New York city and state sales taxes will be added to your bills, unless you are exempt by law."

While the auctioneer spoke, Sam leaned forward and picked up the key ring. He dropped it casually into his jacket pocket.

"Now we begin with lot number one—the Matisse drawing."

A Crispin's employee brought the small, framed drawing out onto the stage, and a murmur of appreciation rose from the crowd. Brooke stood holding the telephone, carefully watching the auctioneer. She was flushed and looked quite beautiful. Sam could see her speaking to the client in what he assumed was fluent Italian.

"For this lot," the auctioneer announced, "I have an opening bid of ten thousand dollars."

Hands went up all around Sam. Several other clerks had stationed themselves in the aisles to help spot the bids.

"Yes, I see several bids around the room. Twelve thousand, five hundred . . . fifteen thousand . . . seventeen thousand, five hundred . . ."

The clerk nearest Sam called out, "Twenty thousand dollars!"

The price rose steadily. Sam watched Brooke, a plan taking form in his mind. He was convinced that whatever she had locked in her desk drawer would explain her behavior and the secret fear that she had only hinted at. It might even explain George Bynum's murder. Sam was ashamed of his own duplicity—Brooke had no idea she had dropped her keys—but he was driven by more than curiosity.

". . . twenty-five thousand," the auctioneer called.

"Twenty-seven thousand, five hundred here."

"Thirty thousand!"

The computerized sign above the auctioneer's head automatically registered the bidding in amounts of foreign currency—francs, pounds, yen, lire and deutschmarks—as well as dollars. There were many foreigners in the audience, their eyes glued to the reeling numbers. The competition had narrowed to a Japanese businessman in horn-rimmed spectacles and a pin-striped suit, and a bearded American in a plaid vest who had made the last bid. The Japanese moved his chin almost imperceptibly, and the auctioneer reacted instantly.

"Thirty-one thousand here! Do I hear any other bids? . . . No advances?" He scanned the audience. "Fair warning—the bid is thirty-one thousand dollars . . ." He brought the gavel down with a sound like a pistol shot. "Sold! To the gentleman here."

The Japanese businessman beamed; the American seemed only mildly disappointed. A few congratulations were extended to the winner by people around him, but the sale was quickly forgotten. Already another object had replaced the Matisse drawing on the easel, and attention was riveted on this new potential acquisition.

The auctioneer said, "And now lot number fifty-six, a painting by Dégas, *Madame Henri Rouart*, signed and dated 1884. I have a bid of one hundred and fifty thousand to start."

Hands went up just as quickly as they had when the price had been only ten thousand dollars. Sam realized that he was out of his league. The art and the drama surrounding the sale did not touch him, anyway. He was torn between a desire to know the truth about a woman he reluctantly loved and a knowledge that he would be deceiving her if he used the keys.

". . . two hundred thousand!"

"Two hundred and ten," the auctioneer countered. "Two hundred and twenty thousand . . ."

Brooke was bidding now, slightly nodding her head as she followed the instructions of the client on the other side of the Atlantic Ocean, the telephone held tightly against her ear.

The auctioneer told Brooke, "It's against you." She spoke quickly to the client, nodded, and the price rose by another ten thousand dollars. Brooke turned her back to Sam, totally involved in the task. It was now, Sam thought, or never.

"Sold!"

The gavel came down again, and Brooke turned and smiled at Sam, proud of her victory. He smiled back. The Dégas was carried off the stage and replaced by a contemporary painting that looked familiar to Sam, although he could not identify the artist. Brooke was apparently not involved in this sale. She picked up another telephone and began talking to a new client, preparing for the sale to follow.

Sam kept his seat, listening to the auctioneer. "For this lot, a still life by Jim Dine, I have an opening bid of twenty thousand dollars. . . . Yes, I see several bids . . ."

The price rose to sixty thousand in less than a minute. Then it climbed slowly to sixty-five thousand, sixty-eight thousand, and stopped at seventy thousand dollars. The still life went to a young couple with Florida tans and a casual appreciation of their win. They might as well have been buying groceries, Sam thought.

A tremor of excitment ran through the room as the next lot appeared on the stage—an Impressionist painting that was obviously of interest to Brooke's client and to many other collectors in the crowd.

"For this lot," the auctioneer announced, "the Dubuffet, we have an opening bid of one hundred thousand dollars. Yes, I see many bids . . ."

This time Sam didn't wait. As soon as Brooke turned away, he stood up and left the auditorium. Throughout the auction people had moved up and down the aisles, but the Dubuffet had almost emptied the reception area. Everyone wanted to see the action and the winner. Even the guards peered into the auditorium. One of them left his post and followed Sam toward the door that led to the storage room and, eventually, to Brooke's office.

Fortunately the men's room was located next to the door. Sam entered it and washed his hands in the sink. He splashed cold water onto his face. As he dried it with a paper towel, he told the face in the mirror, "Jesus, this is really dumb."

The guard was gone when Sam emerged from the men's room. He heard the auctioneer bark, "Two hundred and fifty thousand . . . two hundred and seventy-five thousand . . ."

He pushed open the door and stepped into the silent, shadowy cavern of the storage room. Walking quickly, Sam passed among the crates and scattered art objects. The hallway leading back to Brooke's office was dark except for the dull glow of the red fire light at the far end. He walked more slowly, fingering the keys in his pocket. He knew he had very little time.

He located the lock on Brooke's door with one hand. With the other he took out the keys and tested them, one by one, working as quickly as he could in the dark. It would take a lot of explaining if the guards discovered him, but Sam's thoughts were not on them. Someone else who worked at Crispin's had murdered two people brutally and without apparent motive. Sam had a hunch that the contents of Brooke's desk would tell him once and for all who that murderer was. In fact, he would stake his life on it.

He felt the key turn in the lock. He opened the door, and felt his way across the office to the desk.

15

Brooke held the telephone closely and covered her other ear with her hand. The client spoke to her in soft, lilting Italian from five thousand miles away; he was calm—far calmer than she—and appreciative. They had just lost the Dubuffet to an aggressive New York art dealer, but the client didn't blame Brooke for that. He was really interested in the next lot—a painting by Jackson Pollock that had drawn many collectors to Crispin's that night and would undoubtedly fetch the highest price.

The client called Brooke his *eyes*. She had dealt with him before, and she tried to imagine an old man sitting in his *palazzo* in the hills outside Milan, where he owned an automobile factory, trying to get his money out of the country by spending it on works of art in distant New York. He wanted the Pollock very badly, he said. He was counting on Brooke to win it for him.

She tried to put other things out of her mind and focus on the event at hand. Hastily she lit up a Gauloise, watching two porters carry the huge, splashy canvas out onto the stage. There was a hush in the audience and then a rising clamor of voices as people discussed the painting and speculated on what the price might be. Arnold Glimsher was also interested in the Pollock, as was the Japanese gentleman in the blue pin-stripe, the owner of a fleet of tankers, and a regular at Crispin's bigger auctions.

"And now," announced the auctioneer, "we will begin the bidding on lot number fifty-four, the painting by Jackson Pollock. I should have an opening bid of two hundred and fifty thousand dollars."

Brooke's client began to bid immediately. Acting as his agent, she bid three hundred and twenty-five thousand, then four hundred thousand. But the price climbed steadily, with half a dozen serious contenders in the contest.

The client told Brooke to wait. She watched the price climb to six hundred thousand dollars. It stayed there for a moment, with the auctioneer and the other callers searching the room for another bidder. Then the aggressive New York dealer made the characteristic chopping motion with his hand, sending the price to six hundred and fifty thousand dollars. It was twenty-five thousand more than he had to bid, and he assumed that would push out the undecided and timorous.

Brooke's client said, in Italian, "Seven."

She nodded to the auctioneer, who barked, "I have a bid of seven hundred thousand dollars."

The New Yorker was clearly annoyed. He turned around and glanced at Brooke, the bright lights reflecting from his bald head. Then he bumped the price up to seven hundred and fifty thousand.

The others bidders had dropped out, with the exception of the Japanese. To Brooke's—and the New York dealer's—surprise, he bid eight hundred thousand. The New Yorker countered with eight hundred and fifty thousand, and the Japanese settled back in his chair with a decisive, almost angry, shake of the head: he was out of the bidding.

The auctioneer turned to Brooke. She heard nothing but silence and the faint static on the line, followed by a calm command. Brooke quickly nodded.

"Nine hundred thousand!" the auctioneer said, and a collective sigh rose from the audience.

Glimsher chopped the air.

"Nine hundred and fifty thousand dollars!"

Brooke's client said, *"Mezzo."* He was almost whispering. Brooke held up one hand and made a slashing motion, signifying that the usual increase should be halved.

The auctioneer said, "I have a bid of nine hundred and seventy-five thousand."

This time the New Yorker stared at Brooke with genuine hostility. He conferred with his business associate in the seat next to him and pushed the price up another ten thousand dollars. It now hovered just below a million dollars, which would be the highest price paid that evening and a record for Brooke. She waited patiently for her client to make up his mind and then mouthed the words "one million dollars" for the auctioneer.

The sum flashed across the board as he announced it, and applause broke out in the audience. Flashbulbs went off all around the room. People stood briefly and craned their necks for a glimpse of the young woman with the million dollar bid. Brooke knew she was blushing. She turned and proudly glanced in Sam's direction. But his chair was empty; there was no sign of him anywhere in the auditorium.

A dread came over her. She looked down at the papers on the table. Her keys were missing. She looked under the papers without finding the key ring. In the meantime the auctioneer's gavel blows rang through the room as he tried to restore order and continue the bidding.

Brooke's client wanted to know what was happening. Distractedly she explained that the bidding was continuing. She could not believe that the keys were gone. Sam—or someone—might at that moment be looking into Brooke's desk drawer.

"The bid is one million dollars. It's against you, sir," the auctioneer added, "on the aisle."

The New York dealer conferred with his associate. It was obvious to Brooke that the other man did not want to go higher, and a brief, intense argument broke out between them. Then he chopped the air one last time.

"One million one hundred thousand dollars!" The auctioneer turned to Brooke. "It's against you now, on the telephone."

Brooke wanted to hang up and run from the auditorium. All eyes were on her, waiting to see if her client had lost his nerve at last. All she could think about were the keys and the terrible evidence in her desk drawer at the other end of the building.

Her client, seemingly exhausted, told Brooke to try one more time. She nodded.

"One million two hundred thousand on the telephone, now." Even the auctioneer couldn't hide his excitement. "It's against you, sir."

But the New Yorker had had enough. He and

his associate stood amidst the exclamations of disbelief, caused by her bid, and pushed their way out. He cast a final withering glance in Brooke's direction.

"The bid is one million two hundred thousand. Are there any advances?" The auctioneer scanned the room, but it was clear that the competition for the Pollock was over. "Fair warning. . . . Sold!"— and he brought the gavel down—"to the client on the telephone."

Brooke barely heard the applause.

Sam sat at Brooke's desk, the lamp on and the papers that had been locked in the drawer spread out before him. They made no sense to him. However, the cumulative effect was disturbing. Among the papers lay a photograph of a young woman standing with George Bynum. They were holding hands. It had been a charming snapshot that they had taken on an outing, but someone had used a ball-point pen to viciously scratch through the woman's face. The effect of the mutilation was frightening—a kind of murder by proxy.

Sam returned to the letter he had been trying to read. It had been torn into pieces, and he had patiently reassembled enough of the pieces to make out some words—and George Bynum's signature.

Once and for all . . . leave me alone . . . you disgust me. . . . Don't think for one minute you can get away with . . . or I will tell them everything I know about you. . . .

Sam thought he heard a movement in the dark

139

hallway. He waited, his hand on the lamp switch, but he heard nothing else. He tried to figure out what Bynum's note meant. It sounded like a rejection of Brooke, but he could find no woman's name among the scraps of paper.

He fished through the papers again, locating a newspaper photograph that Brooke had been trying to destroy when Sam surprised her. The photo showed a handsome middle-aged man with a dark mustache. It had been taken from an Italian newspaper. Sam could not read the description beneath the paper, but he did recognize the name of Brooke's father. Then he found another photograph. It showed the same man lying in the street, with Brooke kneeling over him. Beneath the photo he recognized the word, *morte*—meaning "death."

Sam heard the sound again. Slowly he stood up and walked toward the door of the office. The lamp behind him cast a long shadow into the hall. His blood froze as a figure crossed from the darkness to the light, confronting him.

Sam gasped. It was Brooke.

"May I have my keys?" she said coldly.

She put out her hand and Sam inadvertently stepped back, afraid of her. He could see the sadness in her gaze.

"Look," he said, "this isn't what you think. All I was trying to do was . . ."

"Are you spying on me for the police?" She stood very close to him. "Is that what you're doing? And what are you going to tell them?"

"Nothing."

"Oh, Sam," she said with what sounded like real despair, "it's too late for nothing."

A beam of light swung through the hall. They turned to see a guard watching them.

"All right, what's going on here? Who are you?" he demanded of Sam.

"It's all right, Leo," Brooke said. "He's with me."

"Are you sure you're all right, Miss Reynolds?"

"I'm fine."

She walked over to the desk, stuffed the papers and photographs back into the drawer, and turned the key.

"Would you lock up, please, Leo? We have to get back to the auditorium."

"You folks go ahead."

Sam followed Brooke down the hall. They crossed the dark storage room in silence. He wanted to ask her how her father had died, and why she had never told him about it. But it was clear from Brooke's manner that she considered their relationship at an end. Sam had hoped the contents of her desk would prove the murderess to be someone other than Brooke, but they implicated her even further.

They emerged into the lighted reception area. Another lot was about to be auctioned off.

Brooke turned to Sam and said, "Goodbye, Doctor." She walked off without waiting for an answer.

Sam let her go. He could understand her anger and resentment. What he had done seemed cheap and dishonest, and yet his reasons had been sound. Now he had more problems to contend with. The contents of the desk had raised more questions than they had answered. How had Brooke's father died? Was there any connection between her father's death and the murder of George Bynum? Who was the woman in the photograph? And most important, who had the torn letter from Bynum been addressed to? It appeared to be Brooke, but why would she have left such incriminating evidence in her desk for the police to find? As afraid as Brooke was of the police, she would surely have destroyed those things days before. One explanation was that someone else had placed them in Brooke's desk. If so, who?

Perplexed and hurt by Brooke's rejection, Sam decided to leave. Just then the elevator doors opened, and Detective Vitucci strolled out into the reception area, a toothpick protruding from his lips. He caught sight of Sam.

"Out for a walk?" Vitucci asked. He seemed to have gotten used to seeing Sam.

"A friend sent me an invitation," said Sam, lying. By now the detective knew Sam was shielding someone. "Working late?"

"Yeah. I found this guy today, a bartender. He said Bynum was in his place the night he was killed, and he was with a woman. He said they had a big fight, she went running out, and Bynum followed her. So, I'm meeting the bartender here to see if he can make an identification. Maybe we'll get lucky, huh?"

He winked at Sam, and strolled into the auditorium.

Sam decided that he wouldn't leave just yet.

16

Vitucci leaned against a marble column in the back of the auditorium and tried to look inconspicuous. So much money and so much class made him uneasy. He told himself that he—Detective Joseph Vitucci—and other policemen like him—allowed these people to enjoy their wealth and to take part in such activities as high-priced art auctions without being accosted by criminals. He was a protector and a pursuer of felons. The knowledge made him feel better about himself, his job, and the shabbiness of his clothes when they were compared with the tweeds and furs that graced the enormous, beautifully appointed room.

He glanced back at the elevator. Dr. Rice was gone; there was no sign of the bartender. Vitucci had sent a squad car to pick him up, in case the bartender changed his mind. Vitucci hoped to close the case that night. His captain and the police chief were both breathing down his neck. If a third murder occurred before Vitucci could make an arrest, he would catch hell.

The auction was a mystery to him. A painting of what appeared to be a man watching several women sew stood on an easel on the stage. The colors were faded and the figures looked blurry to Vitucci, as if they had been painted by a child. He heard the auctioneer say, "Now we come to lot number sixty, a watercolor by Vuillard, signed and dated. I have a bid of two thousand to start."

Did he mean two thousand dollars? Vitucci stared at the figure on the computer board above the lectern. Then he stared at the painting itself. Anybody willing to pay two thousand dollars for a blotchy painting like that had to have more money than he knew what to do with. And apparently there were plenty of people with too much money, for hands shot up all over the room.

"Two thousand, five hundred . . . two thousand, nine hundred," the auctioneer chanted. "Three thousand . . ."

Vitucci saw the uniformed policeman before he saw the bartender. They stepped off the elevator together and looked blankly around. Vitucci caught the policeman's eye and waved the pair over. The bartender wore a Windbreaker and did not look happy to be in such a fancy place.

"Did you bring your glasses?" Vitucci asked him.

"I brought 'em," said the bartender.

He nervously fished a cigarette out of his pocket. But before he could light it, a guard stepped forward and said, "Sorry, sir, smoking's not allowed."

Sam had slipped back into the auditorium without Vitucci noticing him. From where he sat, he could see the detective, a cop, and a short, stocky man that Sam assumed was the bartender. Sam had to get a message to Brooke somehow, to warn her. Even if she had been with Bynum the night of the murder, that did not mean she was guilty. But Vitucci was unlikely to accept that reasoning. If they happened to arrest Brooke then and there, they would probably search her desk as well.

She stood at the telephone table with Gail Phillips and another woman, her back to Sam. She was unaware of his presence and the presence of the police. He had to warn her without Vitucci noticing.

The Vuillard was taken off the stage and replaced by a large painting by Lichtenstein. The auctioneer opened the bidding at twenty thousand dollars, and the price mounted briskly. Sam kept his eye on the trio in the back of the room. The bartender took a pair of spectacles out of his pocket, put them on, and began to look around. It was only a matter of time until he spotted Brooke.

". . . forty-five thousand . . . fifty thousand dollars . . ."

"Sixty thousand!" said a caller in the aisle.

"Sixty-five," countered the caller on the far side.

The price reached seventy-six thousand dollars, bid by the woman in heavy gold chains seated directly in front of Sam. She gazed around, confident that the bid would not be topped. The crack of the gravel would give her more pleasure than attaining the work of art itself.

Sam stole another glance at Vitucci's group. The bartender stood on his toes, staring straight at Brooke. He seemed to hesitate, then pointed, and turned to the detective.

Instinctively, Sam's hand shot up. The auctioneer recognized him, and the price of the Lichtenstein rose another thousand dollars. The woman turned around and glowered.

Now Vitucci and the bartender were talking animatedly. Sam was vaguely aware that the woman was still bidding. He wanted to postpone the end of this contest, or win, so he could send a note with the caller in the aisle to Brooke. But he didn't have sixty-eight thousand dollars. And he had almost won!

The Lichtenstein went to the woman; Vitucci went off in search of an official of Crispin's. Sam sat fidgeting in his seat, hoping the next lot would appear on the stage before Vitucci returned. If only Brooke would turn around! But she was absorbed in conversation with a client.

A clerk brought a sale card from the desk and handed it to the woman. She signed it and handed it back. Sam tried to tug the man's coattail, but he was already hurrying back toward the front of the room.

"This next piece," the auctioneer said, "lot number eighty-five, is a ceramic by Matisse. I need an opening bid of five thousand dollars. . . . Yes, I see several bids around the room."

The price was bumped up in increments of five hundred dollars. This was more in Sam's league, he thought. Again the woman in front of him led the bidding, her jewelry rattling each time she flailed the air with her hand.

Sam raised his hand.

"Seven thousand five hundred dollars," announced the auctioneer. Now he knew where Sam was.

Vitucci returned with a distinguished looking man in a dark suit who was obviously displeased by the presence of policemen in the house. They conferred, and the man shook his head in the face of Vitucci's demand. They would not disrupt the proceedings to get to Brooke, Sam was sure. They would wait for the auction's conclusion, which was close, and then move in on her.

Sam bid again.

"I have nine thousand now," the auctioneer said, "the gentleman in the back row."

The price jumped to eleven thousand; the woman in front of Sam bid twelve thousand. Still watching Vitucci, Sam bid thirteen thousand.

"I have a bid of thirteen thousand. Are there any other bids? . . . Fair warning . . ."

Sam bid again, thinking he had been topped. He noticed that Vitucci had begun to inch down the aisle in Brooke's direction, followed by the official from Crispin's.

"Yes, sir," the auctioneer reminded Sam, "I have your bid."

The woman bid fourteen thousand. Sam immediately bid fifteen. People had begun to take notice of his passionate bidding. Sam was obviously a Matisse fanatic who must have the ceramic at any price. Even the woman was no match for him.

"Do I have any advances on fifteen thousand dollars? . . . Fair warning. . . . Sold to the gentleman in the back row."

Sam took out his pen and quickly wrote across the back of his program:

Don't look up. The police are coming to question you. Get out the back way. Meet me in ten minutes at 75th St. and Madison. Sam.

* * *

He folded the program and placed it on his lap. It seemed to take the clerk years to bring him the sale card. Vitucci had already started down the aisle, but the official put a restraining hand on his arm: the auction wasn't over yet.

"And now to the last lot in tonight's sale," said the auctioneer. "Lot number eighty-six, a painting by Franz Kline. For this I would like an opening bid of ten thousand dollars. I see I have several."

The clerk arrived with the sale card. Sam took it from him, quickly signed it, and handed it back.

"Just a minute, please."

He slipped his program to the man. "Would you please give this to Miss Reynolds?"

Those people who had bought nothing all evening, or who had not bid, were eager to get in on the last sale. Vitucci waited in a sea of hands, watching Brooke, the Crispin's official stationed right behind him. Sam thought Brooke would notice them, but she was involved in the bidding herself.

"Fourteen thousand . . ."

"Fifteen!"

". . . I have a bid of sixteen thousand dollars."

"Seventeen!"

The clerk paused at the end of the aisle to pass another bid to the auctioneer. Sam could have strangled him. Then he leaned over and placed the program on the table in front of Brooke. She nodded to the clerk but was too involved with the client to read the message.

Sam couldn't believe what was happening. Vitucci was inching forward, the auction was almost over, and Brooke remained totally unaware of the danger. Sam stood up, trying to will Brooke to read what he had written.

"I have a bid of twenty thousand dollars."

"Twenty-one thousand!" It was Brooke's bid.

"Twenty-two thousand!"

The price hung there for several seconds while Brooke carried on an intense dialogue with her client. Then she shook her head at the auctioneer and hung up the telephone. She seemed exhausted, and she had every right to be. *Look down,* Sam thought. *Read the message!*

"Are there any more advances?" the auctioneer asked. "Fair warning. . . . Sold!"—and the final crack of the gavel brought the assembled collectors, art patrons, and curious bystanders to their feet—"to the gentleman on the aisle."

Brooke listlessly picked up Sam's program. Her gaze wandered over it; at the same time Vitucci pushed against the crowd of people on their way out.

Read!

"Thank you, ladies and gentlemen. That concludes our sale for this evening. We will continue with the antiquities section tomorrow at ten A.M. Your bills and purchases are ready on the floor below . . ."

Brooke finally read the note. Her expression remained the same, but Sam knew that she had understood. She rolled up the program, slipped an arm through the strap of her purse, and got up from the table. She glanced once in Sam's direction, with what he thought was a look of gratitude, and then walked calmly toward the door at the back of the stage.

Vitucci called out to her, but no one heard him over the din of up-raised voices. The detective fought against the current of bodies, leaving the chagrined Crispin's officials in his wake. Sam saw the uniformed policeman push down his aisle, also struggling to reach the stage.

Brooke nodded to the porter who was removing the last sale item, and then disappeared through the doorway.

Sam heaved a sigh of relief. Vitucci and the cop were still sixty seconds away from the door.

He stepped out into the aisle and let the crowd carry him toward the elevators.

For twenty minutes he stood on the corner waiting for her to appear. People poured out of Crispin's and were whisked away by limousines and cabs waiting in a line that snaked up the side street. The lights on the top floor of the auction house went out one by one.

He stepped into the telephone booth and dialed Brooke's number. Each time the telephone rang, Sam came closer to the realization that Brooke was not going to meet him. He was not to be trusted; she was on her own now.

He stepped back out onto the street. The crowd in front of Crispin's had dispersed, and the spotlights over the entrance died suddenly. Employees came out the side door in twos and threes, talking cheerfully, still excited by the evening's sale. It wasn't often, Sam supposed, that a work of art brought a million dollars. Brooke's victory had been short-lived.

The cop and the bartender appeared. They got

into a squad car and roared across town. Vitucci was still inside. Sam wondered if they had caught Brooke after all, if the detective was questioning her in her office. If Brooke had tried to retrieve the papers and photographs from her desk, there was a good chance Vitucci had found her.

Sam crossed the street. There was nothing else to do except return to the third floor and offer to help in any way he could.

Two couples emerged from the side door. Sam recognized Gail Phillips with another woman and two men. They were discussing where to go for a snack. Sam approached the group, and touched Gail's arm.

"Excuse me," he said.

She turned to him. "Oh, hi." She sounded more reserved than he remembered her being.

"Could I speak with you just a moment, please?"

The others looked curiously at Sam. But he took Gail's hand and led her a few paces away.

"I'm trying to locate Brooke Reynolds," he told her. "Do you have any idea where she is?"

"No, I haven't seen her since the sale. The police are looking for her, too," she added.

So Vitucci hadn't found her.

"Have you tried her apartment?" Gail asked.

"Yes. She's not there."

"Well, why don't you try her at the office tomorrow? She gets in between nine-thirty and ten, usually."

Gail smiled sympathetically and started to go back to her friends. Sam could tell that she didn't want to get involved. But she was the closest thing

Brooke had to a friend at Crispin's and probably knew where Brooke had gone.

"Wait a minute," Sam said, hearing the urgency in his own voice. "I've got to talk to her. It's very important."

Gail studied him for a moment, trying to make a decision.

"Please," he said.

"Oh, God, she's gonna kill me for this." Then she shrugged. "I know her family has a house out on Long Island. She goes there sometimes."

"Where?"

"In Glen Cove. I think it's on Woods Lane . . . Woods Street—something like that. I think it's on the beach, near the . . ."

But Sam didn't let her finish. "Thanks," he said, and he turned and hailed a cab.

17

Vitucci sat at Brooke's desk, the contents of the drawer spread out before him. Mr. Dorance, Crispin's manager, stood just outside the circle of light shed by the desk lamp; his silence was full of disapproval. He didn't like Vitucci going through the desks of his employees, but there was nothing much Dorance could do about it. If he had refused Vitucci permission to search the drawer, it would have looked like Dorance—and Crispin's—had something to hide.

Apparently they had plenty to hide, Vitucci decided. The bartender had identified Brooke Reynolds as the woman who had an argument with George Bynum the night he was murdered. Brooke Reynolds had given him the slip, probably acting on the advice of the psychiatrist. It had taken Vitucci a while to put those two together. A plainclothesman had followed Dr. Rice to the Reynolds woman's apartment building the night before, then followed the pair of them to a fancy restaurant on the West Side, and from there to the good doctor's apartment. Vitucci suspected that it was Brooke Reynolds that Rice had followed into Central Park the night of the second murder. For an employee of a classy place like Crispin's, she showed up in some strange places.

Vitucci was ninety-nine per cent sure that Brooke Reynolds was a psychopathic murderer. He had one reservation, though, and it concerned Sam Rice. Brooke was not his patient, so Rice was not obliged to protect her or to claim confidentiality. Yet Rice had systematically lied to Vitucci about the woman, placing himself in some jeopardy. He had also taken the suspect to bed, if the plainclothesman's report was accurate. As a psychiatrist, Rice was trained to know a psychopath when he saw one, so why would he risk making love to a woman who might carve him up during the night? Like most psychiatrists, Vitucci thought, Sam might be a little bit crazy, but he sure wasn't stupid. Obviously the doctor was not convinced that Brooke was guilty, and he knew a lot more about her than Vitucci did.

He read the letter again that he had assembled out of the bits and pieces he had found in the drawer. Bynum got around, all right. He had trouble getting rid of his women, but the question remained, which one?

. . . Don't think for one minute you can get away with . . . or I will tell them everything I know about you.

He looked again at the newspaper photos. Vitucci had learned enough Italian from his grandmother to put that story together. Brooke Reynolds's father had been killed in a fall on the streets of Florence when his daughter was with him. Judging from the appearance of her father, he had been about the same age as Bynum when he died.

Vitucci picked up the telephone and called the dispatcher at CID. "Put out an All Points Bulletin on a white female, early twenties, named Brooke Reynolds." He gave the dispatcher a full description, as well as the suspect's address, and hung up. An APB would bring her in if a cop happened to stumble over Brooke in the street; otherwise, Vitucci would have to find her.

Of all the things he had discovered in the drawer, the photograph of Bynum with a woman interested him the most. Her face was scratched out, but what remained was very nice indeed. She could have been any of a dozen women at Crispin's that Vitucci had questioned. Her clothes were tasteful, but the most distinctive thing she wore was a charm bracelet.

Vitucci held the photograph up to the light. It was no ordinary charm bracelet—the pendants were heavy and obviously valuable. He was sure he had seen that bracelet before.

Dorance said peevishly, "Well, Detective?"

"Well, what, Mr. Dorance?"

"How long before you'll be through here?"

"Oh, I'm through now. But my friends haven't even gotten started."

Vitucci slipped the photograph into his pocket. He picked up the telephone again and called Forensic. He gave the sergeant on the night shift the name and address of Crispin's and told him what he was looking for. "Print everything on the desk and then bag it," Vitucci said. "Make sure your boy prints the insides of the drawers, too."

He hung up and told Dorance, "Please lock up

this office and have the guard wait outside until they get here. Don't let anyone else in."

"This is highly irregular," complained Mr. Dorance.

"So is murder," said Vitucci.

Brooke stared out the window of the train at the endless lines of traffic. It was like rush hour in the middle of the night, the thousands of cars moving in and out of the city without regard for time. The constant movement of people and machines had been one of the most surprising things she had encountered when she moved from London to New York. In Europe, the cities slept between midnight and dawn.

The high-rise apartment buildings of Queens gave way to the featureless sprawl of suburban Long Island. Brooke had caught the last train east. She had had to change at Jamaica, standing with a handful of other passengers on the windy platform. She had scrutinized each of them, to see if they were following her. She had never felt more alone. What should have been a day of triumph— and happiness—had become part of her ongoing nightmare.

It was hard to believe that she had woken that morning in Sam's bed. She thought he was an ally, as well as a lover, and then she discovered him going through the things in her desk. Brooke's outrage had been a cover for the deeper distress she felt. He had betrayed her; there was no one she could trust now.

Brooke felt that she had been pursued for most of her adult life. To love and to trust others—even members of her own family—only led to unhappiness, even danger. In a strange way, Brooke had foreseen the things that were happening to her now.

There was one bright spot in the otherwise alien landscape: at least Sam had warned her. She had a few hours to herself, before they found her.

The old train shuddered as it rolled toward the north shore.

Sam walked around the corner, to the apartment building next door to his own. The parking garage in the basement closed at eleven P.M., but fortunately the door was still open. The old man who ran the lot at night was dozing in the filthy cubicle at the top of the ramp, the unlit stump of a cigar still pinched between his fingers. He came awake with a start when Sam opened the door, but his fear quickly turned to sullen disapproval.

"I'm closed," he growled.

"I need the car; it's an emergency. I'm a doctor," Sam quickly added, as if that made any difference to the old man. Sam pulled out his money, and peeled off a ten-dollar bill. "Please."

The man took the money reluctantly. Grumbling, the cigar returned to its slot between his teeth, he led Sam down the ramp. It was crowded with cars parked bumper to bumper; others were jammed into spaces so tightly that the doors would barely open. Sam spotted his Volvo station wagon—new, but covered with the grime of the city, and rarely used—pinned in by at least two other cars. The car had been Sarah's idea—a way for them to escape from the city on weekends, to the mountains or the seashore. But her acting and Sam's work usually kept them in Manhattan on Saturdays, and on Sunday it had been much easier to read the newspapers and go out to eat in the neighborhood than to drive a hundred miles. It cost Sam a small fortune to keep the car in this damp, smelly place, and yet he was reluctant to sell it. Now he was glad he had it.

Still grumbling, the old man moved the other cars. Sam hoped the Volvo had gas in it. He was grateful that he did not drive a larger American car, or he would never have been able to maneuver it up the crowded ramp.

He squeezed into the driver's seat and turned on the ignition. Fortunately the motor turned over on the second try. There was enough gas to get him to one of the all-night stations off the Long Island Expressway.

It took him twenty minutes to get the car out onto the street. He pulled up for a moment under a street lamp to mentally map his course. He would take the Fifty-ninth Street Bridge, crossing the park just a few blocks from the scene of Bynum's murder.

He felt like a traveler in a strange land, without bearings or any knowledge of the journey's end.

Vitucci left his cruiser next to a fire hydrant on East Eighty-first Street and climbed the steps to the door of Brooke's disreputable-looking apartment building. There was no answer when he tried the bell, as Vitucci had anticipated. There was no button to push to call the superintendent of the building, but Vitucci had seen the flickering gray light from a television screen between the curtains on the basement window.

He went down to the door beneath the steps and pounded it for five solid minutes. Finally it opened a crack, and he saw a grizzled face behind two strong chains, squinting up at the light.

"Go away," the superintendent said, "or I'm calling the police."

"I am the police." Vitucci shoved his shield into the crack in the doorway, and let the man study it. "I need to get into Miss Reynolds's apartment."

"You got a warrant?"

"No, but I've got some ideas about safety-code violations in this dump. Open the door, or you're going to be out of a job."

The superintendent did as he was told. He slipped into a grimy parka and led Vitucci upstairs. The building had probably once been beautiful, but now it gave Vitucci the creeps. He could too easily imagine a psychopath living there.

The super took out his key ring, and after a lengthy search for the right key, opened the door to Brooke Reynolds's apartment. Vitucci turned on all the lights. The place reminded him of a museum, full of the same kind of stuff they had been selling at the auction—all of it old and, he supposed, very expensive.

"I'm just looking for Miss Reynolds," he explained to the super. The search for evidence would come later, when they had a warrant. He moved slowly through the rooms—parlor, bedroom, and kitchen—opening closet doors, looking under the bed, and even checking the pantry. There was no one in the place. He doubted that she had returned there after the auction, since there was no winter coat in the closet, and the rooms had been completely dark.

Vitucci went back down the stairs. He thanked the super and told him to call the precinct station if the young woman showed up the next day. A cruiser was parked at the end of the street, Vitucci noticed, an unmarked compact with two plainclothesmen inside, as he had requested. If Brooke Reynolds returned, they would collar her, but Vitucci was almost certain she wouldn't return.

He got into his own cruiser and sat for a while in the dark, thinking. Where would a good-looking young woman go if she was on the run? She would go to a man, he decided.

He drove west, through Central Park and up Columbus Avenue. He parked at the entrance to Dr. Rice's apartment building, where there was an awning. The brass number plate gleamed in the light from the street lamps. A uniformed doorman sat on the other side of the glass, watching the detective, and he opened the door when he saw that Vitucci would not go away.

"I'm here to see Doctor Rice," Vitucci told him.

"He's not here."

"How do you know?"

The doorman eyed Vitucci. He didn't have to be told that he was a policeman.

"I saw him go out half an hour ago. He ain't been back."

"Did he have anybody with him?"

"Nobody," the doorman said.

"Anybody in his apartment?"

The doorman shook his head. "Ain't been anybody up there all night."

Vitucci hesitated. The man was probably telling the truth. If Rice was protecting the woman, he wouldn't bring her there.

He went back to his car and thought some more about his quarry. If a good-looking young woman did not go to a man, then she would go to a friend. Her friends probably worked at the same place she worked. Vitucci took out his notebook and opened it. With one finger he ran down the list of women he had questioned. Two of them lived within a few blocks of Brooke Reynolds, and he turned on the light in the cruiser to make out the exact addresses.

It was after midnight. It had been a long day for him, but he didn't feel the fatigue that usually went with routine police work because he was close to the end of the investigation. He fished the photograph out of his pocket and stared at the faceless woman.

18

Gail Phillips could not concentrate on the conversation around her. She and the other employees from Crispin's with whom she worked often ate a snack at one of the bars on Lexington Avenue. They were gay occasions, full of fun and gossip, but the appearance of the police at the auction earlier had cast a pall over the occasion. Instead of discussing the fact that Brooke had helped bid a painting past the million dollar mark, they all talked about her as a possible suspect in the murder of George Bynum.

Gail's head ached, a sign of stress. She had the reputation for being amusing and carefree, and maintaining that facade could be exhausting on days like the one she had just been through. She had suspected for a long time that Brooke and George were having an affair, and Brooke's admission of the fact that morning had not interested her. Gail had her own problems.

"You were friendly with Brooke, Gail," said Celeste, who worked with her in the public relations department. "Did you ever get the idea that George was chasing Brooke?"

Gail pretended to consider the question. "I don't guess so, but nothing would surprise me."

"Brooke's good-looking enough," said Larry Clements, the bright young star of the accounting department, "to have an affair with about anybody she wanted."

Gail felt the stirrings of jealousy. She recognized the danger signal and said carefully, "Brooke's gorgeous, all right, but awful quiet. I sometimes wondered if that quietness wasn't hiding something."

The others looked at her with interest. There was no need to say anything more: they were already suspicious of Brooke.

Gail took some money from her purse and dropped it among the empty plates and half-filled beer glasses.

"I'm exhausted," she said. "I'm going home and sleep until noon tomorrow. Crispin's can do without me."

"Watch out for people with knives," Larry Clements called after her, and he and the others laughed nervously.

Lexington Avenue was practically deserted. She stood and hailed a cab, unconcerned about the lateness of the hour and the fact that she was a woman alone on the street. Gail had never been afraid of physical harm, being strong and assertive herself. For her, terror lay in the mind, and Gail prided herself on control.

She rode uptown, her fists clenched in her lap.

She paid the driver and crossed the pavement toward the door of her apartment building. As she entered the vestibule, she saw a man climb out of a parked car and hurry toward the entrance. Before she could get the door unlocked, the man was standing next to her.

"Miss Phillips?"

Gail turned to confront him, and saw that it was the detective from Homicide.

"I was wondering if I could take a few minutes of your time."

"My God," Gail said. "You scared me to death." In fact, she was wondering what on earth he wanted.

"I'm sorry to bother you this late, but it really is important." The detective smiled and added, "It's about Miss Reynolds."

"Sure."

She waited for him to ask his questions, but it was obvious that he wanted to go inside.

"You want to come up?" she asked, pretending that it didn't matter to her.

He nodded, and they entered the building together. Riding up in the elevator, Gail's heart pounded.

"I forget your name," she said. "I'm sorry."

"Joseph Vitucci."

"Did you find Brooke, Mister Vitucci?"

"Not yet, but we will. I want to talk to you about her, Miss Phillips. I think she was having an affair with George Bynum."

"It's possible."

"I also think she murdered him."

They stepped out into the corridor, and Gail let the detective into her efficiency apartment.

"Even if they were having an affair," Gail said, "what makes you think she killed him, for God's sake?"

165

"I found some stuff in her desk at work. If it checks out the way I think it will—fingerprints and all—then she's our guy."

"What kind of stuff?"

"A letter, some newspaper clippings, and a photograph."

"What kind of letter?" she persisted.

"From George Bynum to a woman. He was telling her that he didn't want to see her again. Sounded like he hated her."

Gail said nothing.

"I don't know who it was written to."

"It must have been the person who killed him," she said. "The woman was probably very much in love with George. And when she found out what he was like, it broke her heart."

"I wonder why she kept the stuff in her desk," Vitucci said absently. He took a photograph out of his pocket and held it up for Gail to see. "Have any idea who that woman might be?"

"No," she lied. "If you don't mind, Mr. Vitucci, I'd like to take off this make-up."

"Oh, go right ahead."

Gail went into the bathroom, leaving the door slightly ajar. She heard him say, "I guess somebody else could have put the stuff in her drawer."

"Why would they want to do that?"

"To incriminate her, I guess, although that seems unlikely."

Gail looked at herself in the mirror; it was the face of a stranger.

Vitucci couldn't sit still. He paced the room, glancing at Gail Phillips's framed print and silk flowers on the coffee table. There was an anonymous quality about the apartment, as if anyone could have lived there, that was very different from the intensely personal objects he had seen where Brooke Reynolds lived. They were obviously different types, though both wore expensive, tasteful clothes. Vitucci had checked out Gail Phillips's jewelry as soon as they had entered the lighted elevator. She was not wearing a charm bracelet, which didn't surprise him. Maybe he had seen it on Brooke Reynolds's wrist the first time he came to Crispin's.

"The way it looks to me," he said, speaking loudly so she could hear him in the bathroom, "Brooke Reynolds and Bynum were having this big thing. Bynum got interested in someone else and was trying to dump her. He gives her the usual song and dance, et cetera."

He strolled into the tiny kitchen and began to open cabinets, idly searching for something to eat. He took out an already opened package of potato chips and popped one into his mouth. He could tell that Gail Phillips had no interest in food. A jar of instant coffee stood on the sink. The only pot on the stove was used for heating water. There were few spices in the cabinet, which meant she didn't do much cooking, and no fresh vegetables. In the freezer, Vitucci found a stack of frozen dinners caked with ice. A butcher knife had been left there.

He strolled back into the living room.

"Anyway," he said, "to make a long story short, Bynum finds out that this one isn't going to be so easy to get rid of. But before he can get out of the relationship, something snaps in her, and she kills him."

He opened the door to the closet. It was so crowded with coats and dresses stored in hanging bags that nothing else would fit. Among the boxes stacked on the closet shelf sat a thick photo album with a red leather cover.

Gail disagreed with his analysis. "No, I don't think so," she said, speaking slowly and thoughtfully. "I don't think it could have been like that. I think all her life, everyone she had ever cared about had betrayed her, had let her down."

Vitucci lifted the photo album off the shelf. The smell of the new leather was very strong. Cradling the album in one arm, he began to leaf through it. At first he couldn't believe what he was seeing: every photograph was of George Bynum, or of Bynum with Gail, obviously taken with an automatic shutter.

"I think she had made a kind of peace with that," Gail was saying, "and then she met George Bynum . . ."

Vitucci grunted, as if he agreed with her, and edged deeper into the closet. There were photos of Bynum on the beach, Bynum perched on a fence in the New England countryside, Bynum at the Central Park Zoo.

"You have no idea how charming he could be. He knew everything . . ." Gail's voice sounded far away and dreamy. "He had a way of promising all sorts of things, without ever saying a word. And I think, even though she knew he was married, and even though she knew right from the start that it would never work out, she probably thought that was okay."

The album baffled Vitucci. Why would Gail

Phillips collect photos of George Bynum? Then he saw a photo of them standing together on a covered bridge at the edge of plowed fields, both of them smiling at the camera, Gail looking pretty and uninhibited. They were holding hands.

"Probably when she found out that he had been lying to her all along, it was more than she could take. It probably broke her heart . . ."

Vitucci took the photograph out of his jacket pocket and held it next to the one in the album. The photos were not identical, but the similarity between the two women was unmistakable. They both wore charm bracelets. The woman with the scratched-out face was not Brooke Reynolds, but her friend and associate, Gail Phillips.

He closed the album, full of the warm glow that always came with the sudden resolution of a crime. Vitucci's instincts had been stronger and truer than his rational side, leading him to the murderer by an indirect route.

Carefully he replaced the album on the shelf. He wanted his hands to be free during the next few minutes. He turned back toward the room and saw the dark shadow too late. Gail had been watching him, standing very close, waiting for him to turn. Both hands were raised high above her head, gripping a knife. In that first moment of terror Vitucci saw a face that was almost unrecognizable, distorted by insane rage, her eyes bulging, her mouth set in a hideous grin.

The first blow struck him high on the shoulder, the blade digging painfully into his flesh. Although she was strong, Vitucci was stronger and could have wrestled the knife from her. But he stumbled among the shoes on the floor of the closet and fell back among the coats. This time she stood directly over him and brought the knife down with all her strength, the blade slipped past Vitucci's upraised arm and into the side of his neck. He felt no pain this time, just the shock of the blow, and the sensation of being strangled.

He turned and tried to crawl away among the coats. He felt another blow on his back, driving the breath from him, and then another. He lay still, content to let his life slip away.

She stabbed again and again, driving the blade home with all her strength. The body she punished did not, in her mind, belong to a detective or a psychiatrist, or to George Bynum—it belonged to Brooke Reynolds, the cause of all Gail's unhappiness. She slashed at the neck in an orgy of destruction, until she was gasping for breath, and the coats and the wall of the closet were smeared with blood.

She rocked back on her heels, moaning. Vitucci lay with his legs protruding into the living room, his eyes wide and staring. She left him and carried the butcher knife into the bathroom. She hastily rinsed the blade and slipped the knife into her handbag. Then she washed her hands.

She walked back out into the living room. Stepping over the body of the detective, she took her coat from the closet, calmly checked to see that it had no blood on it, and slipped it over her shoulders. She opened the handbag containing the knife to make sure she had her car keys.

The little black monitor on Vitucci's belt began to beep. Someone at police headquarters was trying to reach him.

Gail went out, locking the apartment door behind her.

19

Sam drove east on the Long Island Expressway after buying gas at an all-night station in
Queens. The bedroom communities blended together at first in a continuous world of street lights.
Then stretches of dark, somnolent countryside began to appear. Soon he was traveling almost alone
on the white concrete ribbon, a few headlights float-
ing eerily on the horizon, the green, iridescent high-
way signs rising up out of the gloom to mark his
progress.

He turned north at the Glen Cove exit. As he
approached the ocean, he could see beautiful old
homes sitting far back on well-tended lawns. Hedge
rows ran like leafy walls along the borders of the
property. If Brooke's family owned a house here,
then they were undoubtedly rich. Brooke had the
manner of someone with a privileged upbringing yet
at the same time seemed alone and curiously vulnerable. Sam wished that he knew more about her,
that he had some frame of reference other than a
murder investigation in which to think about her
—about *them*. In spite of the evidence against her,
Sam's instincts told him to trust and to help her. If
only he knew he was right in following those
instincts.

He stopped at a telephone booth outside the post office and got out of the car. The telephone book was intact. In the light of the street light he found the right page and ran his finger down the listings until he located a Reynolds on Woods Lane.

He got back in the car and sat for a moment, looking up at the moon. It was huge and pale yellow, hanging above the sleeping town, both ominous and beautiful.

He drove along the road that bordered Long Island Sound. Occasionally he glimpsed the water between the houses and the dazzling reflection of the moon on the inky black surface. Most of the mailboxes had no numbers, just the names of the families living in the houses. Many of them were empty that time of year, opulent vacation homes used only on the weekends by wealthy people living in the city. In spite of the beauty of the setting, the road and the houses had a forlorn, deserted air.

The Reynolds's mailbox appeared in the headlights. Sam turned into the driveway. Trees grew thickly on both sides, part of an elaborate landscaping plan. But the grounds were no longer well tended. He parked beneath a towering pine tree and stepped out into the gravel. There were no other cars. If Brooke had come there, she would have hired a cab from the city or walked from the railroad station. He couldn't believe that she was really there.

The house looked vaguely familiar, fully illuminated by the moon. A trellis ran down to the door, covered with vines. The weathered cedar shakes on the side of the house gleamed like silver; the glass French doors and the windows were dark.

174

The sloping roof and carved, hand-painted eaves reminded Sam of houses he had seen in Switzerland. Beyond the property and far below it, lay the dark expanse of the Atlantic Ocean.

He started toward the back door. A greenhouse had been attached to the house; it was full of shadows. A white cat was perched on the roof of the breezeway, watching him with infinite patience. As soon as Sam saw the cat, he remembered. This was the house from Bynum's dream, the nightmare place where Bynum had been stalked by a little girl who became his angel of death. Sam could not repress a shudder. Bynum had obviously been there before him.

He knocked on the door, softly at first, and then more forcefully. No one came to investigate. He started to open the door, and his elbow struck a bell hanging from the door frame. It rang forlornly.

The door swung open.

"Brooke?"

There was no answer. Sam hesitated and walked inside. The room was dark except for the moonlight streaming in through the window. Except for him, it was empty. He slowly followed the hallway toward the main part of the house. He peered into the living room, full of the ghostly shapes of furniture covered with white cloths.

"Anybody here?"

The silence was oppressive. He turned to leave, but caught sight of something out of the corner of his eye. He turned back, toward the silhouette of a woman seated at the far end of the room.

"Brooke?"

She didn't move. He stood riveted to the spot,

afraid to approach her, determined not to leave. A cigarette lighter flashed, and in the light of the flame he saw her face, calm and detached.

"Are you all right?"

Still she didn't answer, and Sam's relief turned to real anger.

"Why didn't you wait for me outside of Crispin's," he demanded.

Brooke ignored the question. "How did you find me?"

Sam fumbled in the semi-darkness for a light switch.

"What's-her-name—your friend who works at Crispin's. She said you might be out here."

He located a lamp and turned it on. Brooke seemed to leap at him out of the shadows. She wore the same dress that she'd had on at the auction, which meant she had not even returned to her apartment. She smoked her Gauloise indifferently, watching him through the smoke.

"All right," Sam said. "It was wrong of me to go through your desk. I'm sorry about that. I can understand how you feel." He wondered if he would ever completely understand her. "It's personal."

"How can you understand how I feel? How can you know anything." She took a long drag on the cigarette. Sam could see that she was very upset.

"You don't know anything about me," she added. "Do you?"

"No, no I don't." He felt the anger return. "I don't know anything about you, because you haven't told me anything. I do know that the police are convinced that you killed George Bynum."

"And what do you think now?"

Sam didn't answer.

"Do you think I killed him, Sam?"

He hesitated and said, "No."

"But you're not sure."

It wasn't fair of Brooke, putting pressure on him when he had no facts to judge by. He walked over and pulled her roughly up from the chair. Brooke offered no resistance. They stood close to one another, staring into each other's eyes, and again his anger drained away.

He released her and began to pace the room. "Now, listen to me, Brooke. On account of you, I'm an accessory to I don't know what—obstructing justice, I guess. I'm withholding evidence. I'm going to get my license revoked, if I don't get thrown in jail first." He remembered the auction. "And on top of that, I just spent thousands of dollars for a painting I don't even like!"

Brooke smiled at him. "I love you," she said.

"You do?" He was stunned.

She walked up and put her arms around his neck. Gratefully, Sam pulled her to him. They stood for a long moment, taking comfort in the closeness. Then Sam looked up at the painting above the fireplace, a portrait of a distinguished-looking man wearing a suit and tie. Sam recognized the face from a few hours before.

Gently he disengaged himself from Brooke's embrace and looked around the room. A one-eyed teddy bear sat on top of a box of records that had been packed for storage. Now he was certain the house had figured in the dream of his former patient.

"George Bynum was in this house," he said.

Brooke nodded.

"And that's the man in the clipping." Sam pointed at the portrait.

"Yes, that's my father."

She turned away from Sam and took another cigarette from the pack. He hoped she would finally explain the mystery of her past to him.

"Sam, I don't know how those things got into my desk. All that happened years ago . . ."

"All what happened?"

"My father's death."

"How did he die?" Sam asked.

The memory obviously caused her pain. "He fell from a campanile—a bell tower." She lit the cigarette and added, "In Florence."

"Where were you?"

"I was with him."

Sam was almost afraid to ask the next question. "Was it an accident?"

"I don't know."

Without explaining, she turned and opened the door leading out to the garden. The patio was flooded with moonlight. A flagstone path led beneath the overhanging boughs of pine to a large terrace at the end of the house that overlooked the water.

"I still don't know," Brooke said.

"What happened?"

"This house belonged to my mother." She nodded toward a portrait on the far wall. In the painting, an imposing and beautiful woman sat on a bench in that same garden, wearing a white gown. "I grew up here."

It was Brooke's way of beginning the story of

her father's death. She stepped out into the garden, and Sam followed.

"My parents were separated when I was very young. My mother was very wealthy, and my father was a painter. He had no money at all, so he had to beg her for everything. It was humiliating to watch. When they separated, he went back to Italy—he was Italian—and she . . ."

She paused, her face lifted toward the sky. A few ragged clouds drifted across the moon.

"That's when my mother started to drink," Brooke said. "They never got divorced, though—I don't know why. I was sixteen and always away at school. They called me and told me that she finally drank herself to death. I mean, they didn't say it like that, but that's what it was. I really felt nothing for her—no remorse, nothing. After the funeral, my father came and took me back to Florence with him. I lived there for two years. I was the happiest I've ever been in my whole life. And then . . ."

Sam thought he heard the sound of a car moving slowly beyond the trees. But then it was gone.

"Then in June," she said, "on my eighteenth birthday, I came into my inheritance. They flew all the lawyers in from New York. There were all these documents to sign—it was a sizeable estate. Everything went to me, though, and my father got nothing. And in among all the papers was a letter my mother had written to me not long before she died. In the letter she told me how much she had always loved me, and that she was sorry I had never known that. She said my father had turned me against her, and that it had broken her heart. She said that my father had never loved her, that he was only interested in her money. And she said that he had never loved me, either. He had only pretended to, as a weapon against her. She said she was afraid for me, that I should be very, very careful of him, that he would do absolutely anything to get the money she had left me."

Brooke's eyes glistened. Her smile was both beautiful and haunted. Sam was not sure that he wanted to hear the rest of the story.

"I was supposed to go back and sign the rest of the papers that afternoon," Brooke went on, "but I didn't. I went to a chapel near there to be alone. But there were tourists, so I went up to the bell tower. My father followed me up there. He was very upset—he wanted to know what was in the letter. I didn't want to see him and tried to get away, but he wouldn't let me. So I showed the letter to him. He was shaking . . . the paper shook as he read it. When he finished, he folded it up and handed it back to me, and . . ."

Sam knew the memory was taking an emotional toll on her. But she had to finish it.

". . . and he made some joke about my mother, that she was probably drunk when she wrote the letter, or something like that. Then he smiled at me, and I knew she was right about him. He came toward me with his arms out—to embrace me, I think. But there was this look on his face . . . I was terrified of him. I shook him off, and he got furious. He grabbed me and pushed me against this barricade. I tried to pull away, but that made him more angry. He pushed me back against the railing, and I was sure it would break, and then I knew . . .

that's what he was trying to do; he was trying to kill me!"

Sam touched her arm, but Brooke pulled away from him.

"I got wild," she said. "I twisted around and struck him as hard as I could. He let go of me and fell backwards. He must have lost his balance. The railing broke loose, and he fell. He reached out for me and called my name, but I didn't . . . I couldn't move."

Sam put his arms around her and held her tightly against him. He could feel her heart pounding.

"They say he died instantly," Brooke whispered. "There was some scandal at first, but . . . there wasn't even a formal inquest. Everyone knew how much we loved each other."

"And you kept all this buried," Sam said, "until you told George Bynum."

"No, I never told George this."

"But he knew about it."

"Yes, he did."

"But how?" Sam asked.

"I don't know."

Brooke gently pulled away from him. She held herself and shuddered, touched by the cold breeze —or another memory. "I don't know," she repeated and stepped back into the house.

Sam followed her and closed the door. He believed everything Brooke had told him and sympathized with her anguish. He had been afraid that her past contained some terrible secret. There *was* a terrible secret, but it was not Brooke's fault. He was amazed that she had stayed so sane while carrying such a memory with her.

Brooke took another cigarette from the package and lit it. Telling the story about her father seemed to have calmed her.

"When I explained to George that there wasn't any use in our seeing each other anymore," she said, "he told me he knew all about my father. He threatened me, saying he would bring it all up again. I just couldn't bear it . . ."

"And that was here, in this house."

"Yes," she said, surprised. "How did you know?"

"Because Bynum had a dream, and this house was in it. So were you," he added, thinking of the little girl in the white nightgown. "And so was the person who murdered him."

Sam had all the pieces of the puzzle now, but he still couldn't make them fit. He decided to think out loud.

"In the dream, Bynum comes into this house late at night. He walks into a room where all the furniture is covered with sheets." He walked toward the other end of the room, where a black lacquered cabinet stood in the corner. "Against the far wall is a large Oriental cabinet, with a gilded eagle on top. Just like this one."

He opened the doors of the cabinet; it was empty.

"Inside, there's a green box. In the dream, I mean. He takes the box and puts it into his pocket. As he does that, he turns and sees a little girl sitting in a chair . . ."

Sam turned and looked at Brooke, who said, "I don't understand."

"Wait a minute!" He knew he was getting close. "The girl is holding a stuffed animal. While he's watching, she pulls out one of its eyes, and the animal starts to bleed. Bynum gets very scared."

Sam looked around, searching for another aspect of Bynum's dream. The door stood ajar, and a pale light lay over the carpet.

"He turns and sees a door that leads to a long hallway."

"Sam." Brooke sounded alarmed. She was staring at a photograph in a silver frame that sat on top of the piano. In the foreground sat a small girl dressed in white, smiling at the camera. It had to be Brooke.

"Bynum tries to get away from the girl," Sam said, pulling open the door and entering the hallway, "but she starts to follow him. The hallway leads to a large room with more French doors."

So did the real hallway. Brooke followed him into the study, where Sam tried to open one of the French doors. It was locked.

"He tries to get out," Sam said, "but the doors are locked. The child is getting closer. He looks around and sees a staircase . . ."

But there was no sign of a staircase. It was the first element missing from the dream, and Sam felt an immense sense of relief. Once again the evidence had pointed to Brooke as the murderer.

"Well," he said, "there is no staircase."

"Yes, there is."

Brooke crossed the room, and opened a door cleverly hidden in the paneling. Inside, a narrow set of stairs led upward into darkness.

Sam swallowed hard. He passed through the doorway and started up the stairs. "Bynum gets to the top," he went on, "and tries the door, but it won't open." He tried the door at the top of the stairs, but it stuck. "He feels the child getting closer. Finally he gets the door open and steps inside."

Sam shoved, and the door swung open into a bedroom. Double glass doors led out to a balcony. The room had obviously been unused for a long time. Sheets covered the furniture here, also, and the musty smell reminded him of death. Sam wanted to run back down the stairs, but he forced himself to finish the dream.

Brooke was just a silhouette against the glass doors.

"Bynum closes the door behind him," Sam said, "and takes the green box out of his pocket. It slips out of his hand and falls to the floor. . . . He starts to pick it up, and then looks up and sees the little girl . . ."

Brooke said quietly, "It's not a green box."

"What?"

"It's not a green box," she repeated, and Sam could tell that she was upset. "Sam, it sounds like a green box, but it isn't. Gail . . . Gail Phillips, at Crispin's, she has a . . ." Brooke tried to calm herself. "Gail doesn't trust banks, for some reason. She always cashes her paycheck and carries the money with her. Somebody, I forget who it was— it was George!—started calling her 'Greenback,' and the name stuck."

She walked quietly across the gravel, her path illuminated by the moon. She had left her car on the side of the road and her handbag in it. She carried the knife easily at her side; by now she was used to it.

She passed through the garden and emerged on the patio. The light was on in the living room. All Gail could see was furniture covered with sheets, but she knew Brooke was there. This time she wouldn't escape.

Gail had been to the house before. She had followed George and Brooke one night and had to stand outside in humiliation while they made love in a bedroom upstairs. George had paid for that, and now Brooke would pay.

Silently she placed her hand on the handle of the door. It was locked.

Gail pressed her face against the glass.

20

"Oh, my God!"

Sam put his arms around Brooke and held her. The truth had suddenly come to him.

"I have to call the police," he told her.

"Why, what's the matter?"

"Gail Phillips killed George Bynum."

He pulled away and turned toward the stairs. All he could think about now were the horrible slash marks he had seen on the dead man in Central Park.

"Sam, how do you know that?"

"From the dream. Bynum probably thought he had Gail in his pocket, but she got loose." Sam's mother had suggested that. "If I'm not mistaken, they were having an affair when you went to work at Crispin's."

"Gail?"

"Yes. And when Bynum started seeing you, he broke off with her. Or tried to break off. So it's logical you wouldn't know about her. It's also logical that Gail would know about your affair."

Brooke followed him down the stairs. Sam switched on a lamp in the study. A telephone sat on the desk.

"In Gail's mind," he went on, "if it weren't for you, George Bynum would still be alive."

"But that's absurd."

"No, not as far as she's concerned. You are responsible for his death, so you have to be punished."

Sam took Vitucci's card out of his pocket and dialed the number at police headquarters. The desk sergeant answered almost immediately: "Homicide."

Sam said, "Detective Joseph Vitucci, please. This is Doctor Sam Rice."

"Vitucci's not here; he's on the street."

"Well, can you try to reach him?"

"We're having a little trouble locating him," the sergeant said.

"It's very important."

"Okay, we'll give it another try. Hold on."

While he waited, Sam stared out the window, still thinking. The moonlight was really quite strong. The trees seemed to crowd the house, darkly outlined against the sky. For some reason, he felt very uneasy.

Brooke sat down beside him, and Sam took her hand. The other pieces of the puzzle were falling into place.

"Gail's probably had a history of emotional disorders for a long time," he said. "When George Bynum rejected her for you, that probably put her over the edge. She killed him. Now she's become obsessed with you." That would explain how the letter, the newspaper clippings, and the photograph got into Brooke's desk drawer. Gail had done it; she was the headless woman.

"She's tried to make it look as if you did the

murders," Sam said. "And if that doesn't work, she'll probably try to kill you."

For the first time, Sam saw fear in Brooke's eyes. "Wait a minute!" She pushed the long blonde hair out of her face. "*Who* told you I was out here?"

Sam felt a chill. Automatically he looked back at the window. Nothing moved among the massive shadows of the trees.

He hung the phone up.

"I think maybe we'd better get out of here."

They began to move quickly, like a team, both aware of the danger. Brooke switched off the light and taking Sam's hand, led him back down the hall toward the living room.

She crept from window to window, the butcher knife gripped tightly in her right hand. Nothing existed for her but her prey, two frail human beings trapped in the cage of a house. Brooke must be punished, and the psychiatrist, too. Then Gail would be free and well.

Her foot struck a flower pot on the patio, and it rolled on its side. She paused, waiting to see if they had heard. They were getting ready to leave and unaware of her presence.

Gail stepped back from the French doors and raised the knife in both hands. Brooke would come out first, then Doctor Rice.

She would have to be quick.

Brooke gathered up her coat and took a last look around the living room. Sam wished she would hurry. She seemed reluctant to accept the fact that a friend, however slight, could want to murder her.

189

Brooke seemed more vulnerable than she had ever been, and Sam was determined not to let anything happen to her. She had become an essential part of his life without his knowing it.

"These doors are locked," she said. "Let's go out the back way."

She switched off the lamp. Arm in arm they walked down the long corridor, toward the greenhouse, where Sam had come in.

Something moved on a window ledge outside: it was the white cat, following them. It was probably hungry. Sam thought absently how pleasant it would be to live in the house, to dine on the patio and look out over the waters of the Sound. Such a calm, safe existence now seemed unreal, and unattainable.

They stepped out into the night. Sam's elbow struck the bell again, and it rang sonorously. On impulse, he took Brooke's hand and led her directly out into the moonlight. They cut through a flowerbed full of dead stalks left from the summer's flowers. There was already frost on the ground. For the first time, he heard the sound of the ocean—not breaking waves, but the steady lapping of the water at the rocks below the house. Through a space between the trees he could see a buoy light far out on the black water. Beyond it lay the shore of Connecticut and some scattered islands.

They walked out into the driveway, their feet loud in the gravel. As they stopped, Sam thought he heard other footsteps. His mind, he decided, was deceiving him—a direct result of stress. There was no other car in the driveway but his. The Volvo sat at a distance in the shadow of the trees, ready to take them to safety and a telephone. He would call Vitucci from a telephone booth, and the detective could pick up Gail Phillips when he got the chance.

We've made it, Sam thought.

"I forgot something," said Brooke.

"What?"

"My cigarettes; I left them inside."

"We'll buy some on the way out."

"It's too late. Nothing will be open."

She turned toward the house.

"Where are you going, Brooke?" His voice sounded scared.

"Back inside. It won't take but a minute."

He wanted to tell her that cigarettes were bad for her health. He wanted to take her in his arms and force her into the Volvo.

Instead, he said, "I'll start the car. Hurry, Brooke."

She disappeared in the the shadow of the house. Sam turned and started across the stretch of gravel, toward the car. A great sense of urgency had come over him. So far his luck had been good, and Brooke was part of that luck. But time was running out for both of them. Gail Phillips was a psychotic, and Sam knew from experience and from his studies that she could be both insane and extremely crafty. Gail must have been under tremendous stress that night, keeping up her fun-loving facade at Crispin's while trying to implicate Brooke in Bynum's murder. The closer the police got to the truth, the greater the stress became. Sam would tell Vitucci to take another detective with him, when he finally went to arrest her. No one should try to deal with Gail Phillips alone.

*　　*　　*

Brooke had forgotten to lock the door next to the greenhouse. She pushed it open, and walked quickly down the dark hallway. She knew the house intimately and did not need light to find her way. She had been coming to Seacrest, as the house was called, since she was a baby, and it held many wonderful memories for her: the time when her parents were still together and her life seemed so normal. Diving off the long pier below the house; sailing with her father all the way to Sag Harbor; the feel of the hot summer sun on her body, her first taste of steamed lobster. She was glad that Sam had seen the house. It was a part of her, and so was Sam now. He had faith in her against all odds. In the warmth of her feelings toward him, Brooke almost forgot the horror and the danger of the last few days.

A cold breeze touched her cheeks. She stopped on the threshold of the living room. Moonlight flooded in through the open French doors, which had been closed when she and Sam left a few moments before. Brooke thought they had been locked. The curtains swirled softly in the sea breeze, and outside, above the patio, the boughs of the firs and cedars dipped and sighed.

She crossed the room and closed the doors. Sam must not have shut them tightly. Something moved behind her. The lamp on the desk crashed to the floor, and Brooke wheeled and flattened herself against the wall, her fist against her mouth.

The cat streaked across the rug and into the corridor.

Brooke sighed with relief.

* * *

Sam opened the front door of the Volvo and slipped in behind the wheel. He had left the keys under the front seat. He bent forward and felt along the edge of the mat until he located them, and he inserted one into the ignition. The car started instantly. Before that night, it had gone for a month without use. Sam would surely have sold it if someone had offered to buy it. Now, he thought, it's a lifesaver.

Brooke was certainly taking her time. Sam put the car into reverse and backed up toward the trees. He turned on the headlights, and the soft shadows of the moonlit night disappeared in the harsh glare. He drove slowly down to the path leading to the greenhouse and the back door. It stood ajar. Sam could see that the house was in need of repair. It had probably gone unused for years, while Brooke was in London and both her parents dead.

He decided to go in after her. He put the car in neutral and hauled up on the emergency brake. It had never worked properly, requiring a powerful pull to make it hold. He happened to glance in the rear-view mirror as he did so, and saw a smiling face within inches of him—fair hair, arching brows, red lips. For an instant Sam thought that Brooke had returned, before the numbing truth dawned on him.

He lunged against the door. Looking back, he saw Gail lift a hideous, spotted knife and rise up over the seat. It seemed to Sam that everything was happening in slow motion. He grappled with the door handle, but it would not move: he must have locked it when he got in the car.

She stabbed at him, slashing the back of his jacket. Sam raised his arm, twisting in the seat so he could grasp her wrist. But she drove the knife into his shoulder, close to the base of his neck, with a force that took his breath away. The pain was excruciating. He struggled, feeling the life force drain out of him.

Gail kept the pressure on the blade, twisting, digging. Sam slumped forward against the wheel, fighting not to lose consciousness. He recognized the symptoms of shock, but could not stave them off. He heard the car horn blow, so far away. Brooke would be coming out; somehow he had to warn her.

With the last of his strength, Sam held his body against the horn.

He slid into darkness.

21

The blare of the car horn scared Brooke. She had just set the broken lamp back on the desk and gathered up her cigarettes. The persistence of the horn was annoying. Why was Sam so impatient?

She started back down the corridor toward the greenhouse. The horn continued to blow. Her annoyance turned to doubt, and then to dread: something was wrong.

A figure stood in the open doorway, framed by the headlights. Brooke could not see the face, but she could make out the long coat and flowing hair of a woman. The figure slowly raised an arm, and Brooke saw the knife, the blade glistening with fresh blood.

Terror held Brooke in that spot, unable to go forward to Sam, unable to flee. For a long moment she and Gail confronted each other, the car horn blaring mindlessly, in a world without comfort or help. Then Gail stepped forward. With a great effort, Brooke turned and fled back down the corridor, toward the living room. Her feet seemed set in concrete, her hands useless. She imagined the knife blade plunging into her back, passing through her lung and heart, and leaving her dead in her parents' house.

At the doorway, she glanced back. Gail came after her, walking with a curious rocking motion that was almost leisurely and therefore more horrifying. Her sickness seemed evil, gloating on the fear and pain of her victims. Brooke was torn between a desire to help Sam, which meant certain death, and a need to escape.

She careened through the living room, colliding with the sofa, knocking the silver-framed photograph from the piano to the rug. She thought of hiding behind the lacquered cabinet or behind the curtains, but there wasn't time. Already Gail had reached the door, where she stood surveying the room. For the first time, Brooke could see her face. Gail smiled the hideous smile of the deranged, her lips twisted, her eyes wide and glassy, and Brooke groaned in terror.

Gail rushed at her, stumbling over the cord of the broken lamp. She fell on her hands and knees, the knife still gripped in one fist. Brooke ran into the hallway leading back to the study and slammed the door. There was no key. She turned and raced along the hallway, raking a picture from the wall in her haste. It was dark, but fortunately she knew the way.

She flung open the door of the study, and ran to the glass doors that led to the garden on the south side of the house. But they had been locked with a key, and Brooke remembered that the key lay in a jar in the kitchen. There was no way out, unless . . .

She heard the door open at the other end of the hallway. She had only a few seconds to hide. She was vaguely aware that the car horn had stopped blowing, because now she could hear Gail's footsteps, and the frightening sound of her own breathing.

Brooke rushed to the corner of the room and clawed at the little door concealed in the paneling. It had always been difficult to open, and now it perversely resisted her efforts. Brooke closed her eyes, her fingers searching for the crack. She found it and pulled, and the panel swung back. Brooke stooped and stepped inside, pushing the panel back in place just as Gail reached the door of the study.

Brooke stood very still, trying to hold her breath. She heard Gail move heavily through the room. Suddenly light flowed through the crack in the paneling. Gail had turned on a lamp. Brook could plainly see her, standing in the middle of the carpet, searching for her. Brooke wanted to scream. The upraised knife did have blood on it—Sam's blood. She felt horror and guilt, and a fear so overwhelming that she was afraid she would faint. If she did, Gail would certainly hear and find her hiding place.

Gail looked behind the sofa. She turned toward the French doors. Heavy curtains hung on both sides. She stalked them, slashing first one set and then the other. The fact that Brooke was not behind them seemed to further enrage her.

Her gaze moved methodically around the room, passing over the panel where Brooke hid. It stopped at the desk, an old-fashioned roll-top model with a deep well underneath. Gail hurled the chair out of the way and peered under the desk, the knife poised.

Brooke's heart beat so violently that she thought Gail would hear it. The fear—and the chase—had taken her breath away. She tried not to gasp as her lungs fought for oxygen, filling her chest with pain. She knew she must not move or make the slightest sound. Gail stood only a few feet away. She seemed to be listening, her crafty, insane eyes taking in every element of the room. Her gaze moved to the panel. The strip of light falling through the crack onto Brooke's face felt like a spotlight; she was sure that Gail could see her.

She moved closer, so close that Brooke could have touched her. Gail's hair was in disarray from the fall, and there was blood on her hands, and on her cheek where she had brushed the hair from her face.

She stood still, listening.

Brooke was suffocating.

Sam opend his eyes. At first he thought the lighted instrument panel was a starry sky. Gradually he became aware of his surroundings, the car and the residue of terror left by the attack. His shoulder throbbed. He lay across the front seats, in a sticky pool of his own blood. He felt he was waking from a nightmare.

Desperately he tried to clear his head. How long had he been lying there? What had happened to Brooke?

Grasping the steering wheel with his good left arm, he pulled himself into a sitting position. He was light-headed, and nauseous. When he moved his right arm, the pain was almost unbearable.

The wound on top of his shoulder was deep and ugly, but at least it hadn't been fatal. In her haste to get to Brooke, Gail had left him for dead—or at least dying. She probably planned to return, and finish the job.

Carefully, Sam lifted his right arm with his left and held it against his chest. Then he opened the door. His uncertainty about Brooke overrode the pain, and the fear. He felt a terrible anger, a totally irrational desire to destroy the thing that threatened the woman he loved, that threatened him. Sam was no longer a psychiatrist—he was a hunted, and a hunting, animal.

Slowly, he reached across and opened the glove compartment. He hoped it contained a screwdriver or something else he could use as a weapon, but it contained only maps. Sam could have gotten the tire iron out of the back of the car, but that would take too long. Brooke was in great danger. He might already be too late.

He swung his feet out into the gravel. A light burned in the study window at the far end of the house, and the door next to the greenhouse stood open. He stood, steadying himself by leaning against the car and then pushed off toward the path.

A shadow moved across the study window. Sam paused outside the back door, fighting the nausea that threatened to overwhelm him. At least the throbbing shoulder kept him awake.

There was no sound from inside the house.

The knife blade plunged through the crack in the paneling, missing Brooke's face by inches. Gail had heard her breathing, and now she stabbed and chopped at the wood, prying the door open.

Terrified, Brooke turned and fled up the stairs, toward her old bedroom. There was nowhere else to hide. The sickening realization came over her that there was no way out of that tiny room except the stairs. The only other door opened onto a balcony overlooking the Sound. It was a vertical drop from there to the rocks below.

Brooke burst into the bedroom. Hiding would be useless. Frantically, she glanced around for something to defend herself with, but there was nothing that would be effective against a knife. She heard the panel at the bottom of the stairs slam against the wall, followed by Gail's slow, methodical footsteps.

Brooke crossed to the door leading to the balcony and threw it open. The cold sea air shocked her. She stepped to the railing and looked down at the rocks, jagged and bare in the moonlight, touched by the dark water. She felt a new kind of fear. The balcony clung to the side of the house like a nest to a cliff.

She turned back toward the room. Gail stood in the doorway, watching her. Slowly she started across the room, the knife coming up with a horrifying casualness. Gail's smile was cruel and triumphant.

Brooke backed up, onto the balcony. Gail came closer, driving her to the railing. It felt frail to her touch, a thin strip of wood between her and eternity. But it was the knife blade that fascinated Brooke, so close now, and unavoidable. She imagined it plunging into her chest, the jagged edge sawing at her flesh.

Gail came closer. Brooke leaned against the railing, arching backwards, her arms raised against the blow. Gail paused, enjoying Brooke's terror. A thought passed behind her huge eyes.

Gail said hoarsely, "Jump."

"What?"

"Jump!"

Brooke looked down at the rocks below. The thought terrified her, but the knife was more terrifying. The events of the last few days flashed through her mind, leaving her with a single thought: Sam was dead. She was left with nothing but her own unhappy past. Death at that moment seemed at least as acceptable as life.

Brooke turned and gripped the railing.

"Don't!"

The voice filled Brooke with incredible gratitude. She looked back and saw Sam standing in the bedroom, his hand raised in warning, his sleeve soaked with blood.

Gail wheeled toward him. Then she turned and lunged toward Brooke, stabbing savagely. Brooke fell to one side, avoiding the blade, and the weight of the blow carried Gail forward. Off balance, Gail grasped the railing, pivoting her body to stab again.

The railing snapped. Gail teetered over the edge of the balcony. The knife slipped from her hand and fell. She grabbed for the broken railing and missed. For an instant she hovered there, her hand outstretched, Staring at Brooke. On impulse, Brooke reached out and took it. She tried to pull Gail back to safety. But Gail's hand was slippery with Sam's blood.

She plunged, screaming.

Brooke felt Sam's arm around her shoulders. She clung to him. Together they looked down at the still body on the rocks, touched by the cold, clear light of the moon.